Crime in the
Queen's Court

Nancy and Bess decided to join a few other ladies-in-waiting who were sitting on a blanket, munching on biscuits and cold chicken. As the two girls walked across the clearing in their Elizabethan costumes, Nancy's gaze shifted to the woods, and she admired the shafts of soft sunlight falling on the trees.

Then Nancy approached the ladies-in-waiting seated under a large oak tree and said, "Mind if we join you?"

Suddenly, Nancy heard a sharp whizzing noise near her ear. She flinched in surprise and felt a rush of air on her cheek.

Looking to her left, she let out a gasp. Lodged in the tree, only inches from Nancy's head, was a quivering arrow!

Nancy Drew
Mystery Stories

Available from MINSTREL Books

112

NANCY DREW®

CRIME IN THE QUEEN'S COURT

CAROLYN KEENE

A
MINSTREL®
BOOK

PUBLISHED BY POCKET BOOKS

New York   London   Toronto   Sydney   Tokyo   Singapore

This book is a work of fiction. Names, characters, places, and incidents are either products of the author's imagination or are used fictitiously. Any resemblance to actual events or locales or persons, living or dead, is entirely coincidental.

A MINSTREL PAPERBACK *ORIGINAL*

 A Minstrel Book published by
POCKET BOOKS, a division of Simon & Schuster Inc.
1230 Avenue of the Americas, New York, NY 10020

Copyright © 1993 by Simon & Schuster Inc.
Produced by Mega-Books of New York, Inc.

All rights reserved, including the right to reproduce this book or portions thereof in any form whatsoever. For information address Pocket Books, 1230 Avenue of the Americas, New York, NY 10020

ISBN: 0-671-79298-9

First Minstrel Books printing April 1993

10 9 8 7 6 5 4 3 2 1

NANCY DREW, NANCY DREW MYSTERY STORIES, A MINSTREL BOOK and colophon are registered trademarks of Simon & Schuster Inc.

Cover art by Aleta Jenks

Printed in the U.S.A.

Contents

CRIME IN THE QUEEN'S COURT

1

Merry Old England

"O Romeo, Romeo, wherefore art thou Romeo?" Bess Marvin exclaimed with an exaggerated sweep of her hand. Turning to her friend Nancy Drew, she asked, "So, what do you think?"

Nancy smiled as she shielded her eyes from the bright sunshine. "Well, you probably shouldn't give up your day job," she said teasingly.

Bess giggled and tossed her long blond hair. "I guess I just got carried away. This Elizabethan festival makes me feel so . . . so . . ."

"Festive?" finished Bess's cousin, George Fayne, as she guided Bess back into line.

Bess made a face at her cousin. "Well, it does. Admit it," she said to George. "Doesn't just being here make you think of crowns and royalty and England and ladies with long dresses and—"

"Okay, okay," George said, throwing up her hands.

Nancy smiled as she listened to the two cousins. Bess was right, she thought as she moved up in line. There was definitely a feeling of old England in the air. The outdoor pavilion on the outskirts of River Heights had been transformed to look as though it belonged in sixteenth-century London. Its dark wood had been painted to look as if it were made from large stones. From where she was standing, Nancy could see an outdoor theater, part of a backstage tent behind the theater, and a town square with fake building fronts.

There were two rows of trailers parked on the far side of the pavilion. Nancy saw a man in knee-length pants, a vest, stockings, and a hat step out of a trailer. Then a woman in a high-necked dress with puffed sleeves, a tight waist, and full skirt hurried into the trailer. Beyond the trailers was the parking lot, where Nancy's blue Mustang was parked.

For the third year in a row Her Majesty's Players, a traveling acting troupe, had come to River Heights for a week-long festival. This year Nancy, Bess, and George had decided it might be fun to sign up as volunteers for the week.

"Earth calling Nancy," George said, interrupting Nancy's thoughts.

Nancy turned to find herself at the sign-up table at the front of the line. A woman wearing a

2

deep blue, high-necked dress sat at the table, smiling at her. On the table were several sheets of paper—each with a different job description. Most of the jobs had already been taken by other volunteers.

"Good morning, ladies," the woman said pleasantly. "Take a moment to look at the sheets, and then let me know which job interests you."

"Oh, look!" Bess exclaimed, pointing to one of the lists. "'Ladies-in-waiting.'" She looked excitedly at the woman. "Do ladies of the court get to wear dresses like yours?" she asked, admiring the Elizabethan dress.

The woman laughed. "Yes, they do," she answered. "And there are a couple of openings left."

Bess grabbed a pencil and signed her name on one of the lines. "Won't this be fun?" she said.

George rolled her eyes. "Walking around in ruffles and layers all day? No, thanks." But then a different list caught her eye. "Look, there's an opening here to help out the props coordinator. Now, *that* could be interesting," she said, signing her name.

"Props?" Bess said in disbelief. "What do you want to do? Carry a hammer around all day?"

Though Bess and George were cousins, they couldn't be more different, Nancy thought. George, with her short, dark hair and dark eyes, was slender, athletic, and always ready for adventure. Blond-haired, blue-eyed Bess, on the other hand, would rather be watching the action from a safe distance. Bess was forever battling to lose five pounds from her slightly plump frame. And both girls looked completely different from Nancy, who had reddish-blond hair and deep blue eyes.

"So what are *you* going to do, Nancy?" George said, ignoring her cousin's remark.

"I don't know," Nancy said, scanning the sheets. "There's not much left."

"There's room for one lady-in-waiting," Bess suggested.

Nancy looked at the ladies-in-waiting sign-up sheet. The job description sounded fun. Ladies-in-waiting had to wear Elizabethan dresses and attend all events as members of Queen Elizabeth's court. The events included a hunting party picnic, staged duels, dances, the evening play, and more.

"Why not?" Nancy said, signing her name. "It'll give us a chance to see the whole festival."

"Oh, good," Bess said. "It'll be fun to do this together. But just remember," she said, looking concerned, "we're here to have fun—not to look for mysteries."

Nancy laughed. "Don't worry, Bess," she said. Nancy had become known in River Heights as an amateur detective. But while her interest in sleuthing had brought her a good deal of recogni-

4

tion, it had given Bess more than one nervous moment.

"Thanks for volunteering," said the woman at the table. She handed the girls volunteer badges. "Please wear these at all times," she said. "Now you can head over to the theater, where the director, Philip Schotter, will be meeting with the volunteers. And I hope you have a wonderful week." She looked at her watch. "Quick, he'll be starting any minute."

The three girls hurried over to the theater and sat down just as a tall, friendly looking man began speaking. Dressed in jeans and a T-shirt, he looked to be only a few years older than the girls. His brown, curly hair hung down to his shoulders.

"Friends, Romans, countrymen, lend me your ears," he said to the group of about thirty volunteers. "I'm Philip Schotter—better known as Schotter—and I'd like to welcome you to our Elizabethan festival as official members of Her Majesty's Players."

A few people clapped, and Schotter continued with a smile. "We want you to know that we truly appreciate your volunteering. We're a small group, and every bit of help counts.

"The festival officially begins today at noon. It will run for seven days, ending Saturday evening," he continued. "But all volunteers will have a day off on Wednesday. The gates open at noon, and we expect everyone in the troupe—and that now includes all of you—to be in costume by then."

Schotter went on to explain the different spectator activities. They could attend sixteenth-century duels, Shakespearean sonnet readings, hunts, and concerts. They could also learn dances, songs, and games. Every day, in the late afternoon, there would be a performance of Shakespeare's play *Romeo and Juliet.*

"We're very proud to be joined this year by respected actress Martine DeVries, who will be the festival's one and only Queen Elizabeth. The queen and her procession—the ladies-in-waiting and courtiers—will attend meals, the hunting-party picnics, and every play performance. If you're a lady-in-waiting or a courtier, you have a choice of being part of the procession or inter-mingling with the spectators."

Schotter then introduced Josh Forster, the company's creative consultant. "Josh is basically my right-hand man," he said, looking at Josh appreciatively. "You'll be able to count on his expertise in sixteenth-century England's history and literature. Spectators will be asking all sorts of questions, and if you don't know the answer, just ask Josh."

Josh Forster, in his wire-rimmed glasses and tweed jacket, reminded Nancy of a college professor. He began to explain the Elizabethan period to the volunteers. "Queen Elizabeth came to power in 1558. She considered herself to be chosen by God to be the ruler of England, and believed, as many did, that she was responsible only to God," he said.

"This is like being in school," Bess whispered.

"Shh," George whispered back. She had always liked history.

Adjusting his glasses, Josh continued in a quiet, serious voice. "Most of you probably know of a famous citizen of London at that time—William Shakespeare. This week our theater group will be performing one of his most famous plays, *Romeo and Juliet*. This play—"

Suddenly a booming voice rang out. "Josh, I think I should cover this part!" Nancy looked up to see a middle-aged man, whose hair was almost completely gray, appear from backstage.

"You?" Josh frowned. "What do *you* know—"

Schotter, the director, rushed to center stage to smooth things out. "Uh, thank you, Josh, for those important facts," he said awkwardly. "We're running short on time, and I still want to make one more introduction." He gestured toward the man who'd interrupted Josh. "I'm sure most of you recognize the well-known actor Dean Batlan. He'll be playing the part of Romeo."

The man smiled and raised his hands to polite applause.

"That's Romeo?" George said under her

breath. "I thought Romeo was supposed to be a young man. This guy looks middle-aged. And I've never heard of him."

"Well, Dean Batlan's not exactly a teenager," Nancy whispered back. "I think he played Romeo in some major productions a long time ago."

As if he'd heard Nancy's whisper, Dean Batlan began speaking in a loud, confident voice. "Yes, playing Romeo is second nature to me now. In fact, I think that by watching me perform you'll all learn a lot about Shakespeare."

"Thank you, Dean," Schotter broke in quickly. He turned back to the volunteers. "Now, to find out which area you should report to first, check the lists at the edge of the stage. And thanks again for your help."

"Well, that Dean Batlan sure thinks a lot of himself, doesn't he?" George said as the girls went to check the lists.

"He sure does," Bess said, nodding. "I couldn't believe he interrupted poor Josh Forster like that."

"Maybe Dean was starting his theatrical performance a little early," Nancy said. She looked at a sheet of paper with "Ladies-in-waiting" written at the top. "C'mon, Bess. It says here that we have to head over to the costume trailer," she said. The girls said goodbye to George, who was to report to the backstage tent.

Nancy and Bess headed toward the trailer lot and immediately found a large white trailer with a sign on the door that said Costumes.

A petite, dark-haired woman with a clipboard was standing outside the door. "Are you Nancy Drew and Bess Marvin?" she asked, looking at her clipboard.

"That's us," Bess answered.

"Then you're at the right place," the woman said. "I'm Donna Vasquez, the costume manager. Go into the trailer and one of my assistants will help you find costumes."

Inside the trailer, dresses and petticoats hung on racks and on the backs of folding chairs. Screens had been set up to create dressing areas, and several full-length mirrors were propped against the walls. Two other volunteers had just been fitted and were picking out pieces of costume jewelry.

An assistant approached Nancy and Bess. "Are you two playing ladies of the court?" she asked. When Nancy and Bess nodded, she stepped back and eyed them critically. After a moment she turned to a rack of dresses and pulled off a green dress for Bess and an ivory-colored dress for Nancy. "You can change behind those screens there," she said, pointing. "Leave your clothes in the lockers against that wall."

A few minutes later Nancy and Bess came out from behind the screens. "Oh, Nancy, you look beautiful!" Bess exclaimed. The ivory dress set off Nancy's deep blue eyes.

"Thanks," Nancy said. "You look pretty elegant yourself!"

Bess smiled. "I love this style," she said. "I can hide my legs under this full skirt, and the fitted waist isn't even tight on me." She admired herself in a mirror. "It's a lot more flattering than a sweatsuit."

"You two look great," said Donna Vasquez, entering the trailer. "Help yourself to some costume jewelry in those trunks over there. A generous elderly woman, here in River Heights, gave us some of her old pieces. We've added them to our existing collection. They're fakes, of course, but they look like the right time period. The festival regulars have already taken their pieces, but you're welcome to whatever's there."

A few moments later, each wearing a bejeweled pin, Nancy and Bess stepped from the costume trailer. "I feel like we've really stepped into the sixteenth century," Bess said.

"I know what you mean," Nancy said, glancing at her watch. "We have some time before the procession begins. Let's head back toward the town square."

Suddenly they heard a hoarse cry. "Hey, look out! Oh, no—help!"

Nancy immediately ran in the direction of the voice, which seemed to be coming from one of

10

the trailers. As she neared a larger trailer, she was joined by other men and women in costume. She stepped into the trailer and stopped in surprise. Sprawled out on the floor were three men in Elizabethan costume. And on top of them lay a large iron rack filled with spears, swords, axes, and long poles with sharp, oddly shaped blades at the end!

2

A Mysterious Poet

Nancy rushed over to the three men and began to carefully lift the weapons off them. Bess came up behind her and gasped.

"Is anyone hurt?" Nancy asked.

"I—I don't think so," one of the men said shakily. "I know I'm okay."

A few men wearing stage assistant badges helped Nancy clear away the weapons. Together they lifted up the rack and helped the three men to their feet.

"I don't know what happened," said one of the men, who was dressed in a shirt, a vest, knee-length pants, and stockings. "I was just reaching over to take a sword to wear with my courtier costume when the whole thing collapsed."

Nancy saw a stage assistant examining the wall. "Maybe the weapons were too heavy and the rack came loose," Nancy suggested.

The stage assistant shook his head. "I helped put this up—just yesterday," he said. "I know it was secure. We tested it several times."

Nancy turned back toward the scattered weapons and noticed they had one thing in common—they all looked very sharp. The three men were lucky they hadn't been hurt, she thought.

Suddenly a white piece of paper, stuck to one of the spears, caught Nancy's eye. After carefully removing it from the pointed end, she turned it over to find a note written in large, old-fashioned writing:

"O woe! O woeful, woeful, woeful day!
Never was seen so black a day as this."
Shakespeare used words as his weapons of
    choice,
But methinks these weapons have a much
    stronger voice.
And keep this in mind—there's still much
    more fun,
Because my little stunt is only Act One.

"Act One?" said a voice behind Nancy. It belonged to the man dressed as a courtier. Looking over Nancy's shoulder, he read the note out loud to the several people who had gathered there. Nancy noticed that Dean Batlan, Josh Forster, and Philip Schotter had all arrived.

When the man finished reading, Bess gasped.

13

"Do you think someone did this on purpose?" she asked.

"It sure looks that way," Nancy said quietly. Who could be responsible for the falling rack and the note? she wondered. Could one of the cast or crew be playing a cruel joke?

"Well," Josh said, "at least we know somebody's been reading their Shakespeare. The lines at the beginning of the note are from *Romeo and Juliet.*"

Nancy's concentration was broken by the sound of Dean Batlan's loud, theatrical voice. "This is outrageous! That silly note is just an attention-getting device. Obviously someone is jealous of the star of this production—me."

"But you're not the one who got hit—we were!" the courtier protested.

Dean gave him an exasperated look. "But *I'm* the one this really affects. I have the lead role, and I'm being forced to work under these dreadful conditions."

George was right, Nancy thought. Batlan did think he was very important.

"What's happened in there?" came a voice from outside.

The courtier put his hand on Nancy's arm. "Brace yourself," he muttered under his breath. "We're about to face the wrath of Martine DeVries."

Nancy saw everyone in the trailer become

14

tense as an exquisitely dressed woman entered the trailer. Her sandy blond hair was pulled back in a soft bun, and she wore a small crown on her head. Nancy knew she had to be portraying Queen Elizabeth.

Schotter explained to the actress that a rack had fallen over.

"Well, I'm glad *you're* all right," Martine said, narrowing her eyes at Schotter. Her voice was cold and sarcastic. "I'm sure that was the first thing you were worried about." Then, as abruptly as she'd entered, she left the trailer.

Everybody let out sighs of relief. Why did Martine DeVries make everyone so nervous? Nancy wondered. And why had she spoken so coldly to Schotter?

But the director didn't seem bothered at all. He calmly announced that the queen's procession and feast were about to begin. "Ladies and gentlemen of the court," Schotter said, "head over to the pavilion and start lining up. I'll be there once I see about getting this rack repaired."

As everyone began to scatter, Nancy saw Schotter turn to Josh Forster and say, "Can you check into that note, Josh? I want to know what's going on here."

Deciding she'd been given the perfect opportunity, Nancy said, "Excuse me, Mr. Schotter, but I was just going to suggest that I might look into this incident. My name is Nancy Drew, and

15

I'm a volunteer. I do a bit of detective work here in River Heights," she finished.

"Well, I'd really appreciate that, Miss Drew," Schotter replied earnestly. "I have quite a bit of work to do this week, but I'd like to find out what's behind this note."

Josh let out a soft chuckle. "C'mon, Phil, you don't believe that it's anything more than a joke, do you? I think some of our troupe members just got carried away."

"Maybe," Schotter said doubtfully, "but I don't think it would hurt to have Miss Drew here check it out. What do you think, Josh?"

Josh looked at Nancy and shrugged. "Suit yourself," he said. "I just think it might be a waste of your time."

"I'll let you know what I find," Nancy said as she left the trailer.

Outside Nancy found Bess talking to George. "Oh, Nancy, I've just been telling George what happened," Bess said, grabbing Nancy's arm. "I had no idea that a festival like this could be dangerous. Who do you think could have written that strange note?"

"I don't know," Nancy said slowly. "George, do you know if any members of the stage crew were working in that trailer?"

George shook her head. "I've been backstage the whole time. As far as I know, most of the stage crew was there, too. Everybody's pretty

16

busy getting ready for tonight's performance of *Romeo and Juliet.*"

"Maybe somebody from the stage crew went into the trailer at the last minute—just before those three men went in," Bess suggested.

Nancy nodded. "Someone could have gone in to loosen the rack from the wall," she said, "but that note was definitely not written at the last minute. That style of old-fashioned writing takes time. And it's a good way to disguise a person's handwriting. Someone had to have planned it in advance."

"But why?" George asked.

"That's what I want to find out," Nancy said. "But we have to get over to the procession now. We'll see you later, George."

At the entrance to the pavilion Nancy and Bess found a line of ladies and gentlemen of the court, waiting to walk behind Queen Elizabeth as she made her grand entrance into the banquet area. The men wore stockings, breeches, and fitted coats, while most of the women had on dresses similar to those Nancy and Bess were wearing.

Six men were approaching, carrying the queen's litter. The litter was a thronelike seat balanced on two long rods that the men carried over their shoulders. The seat was covered by a canopy held up by four poles.

The men set the chair down and helped Martine DeVries into the lavishly decorated seat.

17

Then, lifting the litter to their shoulders again, they led the procession into the pavilion, where the queen and her "court" were to have their banquet.

As they entered the pavilion, spectators turned and pointed at the queen. Martine DeVries held her head high, giving dignified smiles and nods to everyone—especially to the children.

"Isn't this fun," Bess said. "Look, Nancy, those people are pointing to us. I feel like part of the royal family."

Nancy laughed. "It is fun—as long as you don't have to do it for every meal." They had reached several rows of long wooden tables. The queen had already taken her seat of honor at the head table, which meant that the members of her court could sit down, too. Nancy and Bess sat down at a table adjoining the queen's with a few other ladies-in-waiting.

Platters of food had been placed on the tables. Slices of meat were artfully arranged on one, a variety of cheeses on another. Loaves of bread and biscuits sat in large baskets at the end of each table, and water pitchers were scattered about.

"I'm not sure this is exactly what they ate in Queen Elizabeth's court," Nancy said with a grin. "But this version looks terrific."

"I hope it tastes like twentieth-century food," Bess admitted. "I'm starved."

Spectators began to fill the remaining tables. Members of the troupe dressed as kitchen servants walked around with trays of free samples, but the rest of the spectators' food had to be purchased from a snack stand.

As the food was passed around and eaten, Nancy and Bess had a chance to observe the scenery and spectators.

"Martine makes a pretty convincing queen," Bess said as she watched the woman chatting with a family of seven. "But she didn't seem too friendly toward Schotter in the trailer."

"Everyone seemed to be expecting some big blowup from her," Nancy said.

"Well, you know what they say—actors are supposed to be temperamental," Bess said, shrugging.

"I don't know," Nancy said doubtfully. "Martine seems pretty controlled to me."

"All I know is that playing Queen Elizabeth looks like a lot of fun," Bess said. "Who wouldn't want to be carried around in a litter?"

Nancy smiled and reached for the water pitcher. "We're out of water," she said. "I'll see if I can get an extra pitcher from one of those empty tables."

Walking to another table, Nancy noticed the actor Dean Batlan and Josh Forster, the creative consultant, sitting at the end of the table by themselves. Josh was speaking quietly to Dean. As Nancy reached for a pitcher, she noticed the gray-haired actor begin to rise from his seat. Then, in a low, threatening voice, Dean said, "Don't push me, Josh—I can bring this whole show down whenever I want!"

3

Rehearsal for Disaster

Nancy watched while Dean Batlan walked away from the table. Josh Forster shook his head, and then he, too, got up from the table and left the pavilion.

With Dean Batlan's threat still ringing in her head, Nancy walked back to her table. What was Josh pushing Dean to do? she wondered. And how could Dean bring the show down? More important—why would he threaten to do that?

Her mind raced back to the note that she'd found on the weapons rack—it, too, had threatened harm to the festival. Suddenly she stopped short. Could Dean have had something to do with the falling weapons rack? she wondered. Could he have been trying to "bring the show down" that way?

"Nancy?"

Nancy was startled to see Bess tapping her arm. "Are you all right? You look a little dazed."

Nancy sat down next to Bess. "I'm fine, thanks," she said. "I've just been thinking." She told Bess about Dean's threatening remark.

Bess's eyes grew wide. "What do you think he meant?" she asked.

"I don't know," Nancy said. "It might not mean anything at all. Dean seems to have a pretty high opinion of himself. Maybe he was just boasting." She paused. "But something tells me there was more to that threat. He did look pretty angry at Josh."

"But why would Dean want to hurt the festival?" Bess asked in a confused voice. "He'd be losing his job."

Nancy shook her head. "I think I need to find out more about our Romeo," she said.

Just then a trio of musicians began making their way through the rows of tables. Two of the men played guitars, and the third played the flute. Nancy had been so absorbed in her thoughts that she hadn't noticed that a group of dancers and a couple of clowns had also entered the dining area. They were entertaining the crowd with music, dancing, jokes, and riddles. Nancy and Bess joined in the applause as the dancers finished a set.

Bess sighed. "That was beautiful," she said, watching the dancers pull a couple of spectators out for a spin. "I'd love to learn that kind of dancing. But I'm afraid it takes a little more coordination than I have."

"Don't be silly," Nancy said. "Why not give it a try?" Getting up from the table, she added, "I think I'll wander over to the trailer where the accident happened this morning."

"Okay," Bess said. "I'll stay here and watch for a bit. Be careful, okay?"

But Nancy was already gone.

Approaching the trailer, Nancy was surprised to see George step out the door.

"Hi, there," Nancy said. "What brings you here?"

George grinned. "Guess who had to clean up the mess in there?" she said, pointing toward the trailer.

"Did you have to put the rack back up?" Nancy asked.

George shook her head. "No. J.Z. had us move the weapons to a safer place."

"Who's J.Z.?" Nancy asked.

"Oh, Jerry Zimmer, the props coordinator," George said. "He's the person I've been helping. But what brings *you* here?"

"I thought I might look around a bit," Nancy said, peeking inside the trailer. "But I see all the weapons have been moved."

"Any new developments?" George asked.

23

Nancy told her friend about Dean Batlan's threat.

George raised her eyebrows. "That's funny," she said.

"What do you mean?" Nancy asked.

"Well, from what I've heard, Dean is lucky to be in the show at all," George said. "Apparently, he asked for a lot of money and publicity to be in the festival. But he didn't get it. He's a good actor, but he's not as popular as he was, or, at least, as he thinks he was."

Nancy paused for a moment, taking in George's information. "If that's true, then Dean might think he has a reason to be angry with the festival's producers," she said thoughtfully.

George glanced at her watch. "Sorry, Nan, but I've got to run to the art supplies trailer. The play begins soon, and there's lots to do."

Nancy said goodbye and quickly headed over to the outdoor theater, hoping to catch Dean Batlan before the opening of the play. The afternoon sun created a soft glow on the empty seats and the semicircular stage. Nancy thought that it would be a perfect afternoon and evening for the first performance of *Romeo and Juliet.*

Seeing that the stage was empty, Nancy went into the large tent behind the theater. The tent had been set up so the audience couldn't see what was going on backstage. Inside the tent stage crew members were scurrying around making last-minute adjustments to costumes and scenery. Off to one side Dean Batlan and Joanna Messerman, the actress playing Juliet, were going over their lines as Josh Forster watched from a chair. Nancy recognized Joanna from the picture she'd seen in the troupe's program. The pretty, brown-haired actress was dressed as Juliet, in a simple ivory-colored gown. Nancy moved closer to hear them.

" 'Good night, good night!' " the young actress recited. " 'Parting is such sweet sorrow/That I—' "

Dean Batlan threw up his hands. "No, no, no!" he exclaimed. "That's all wrong, Joanna! You're being too forceful. These lines are supposed to be said delicately."

"Listen, Dean," Joanna said, trying to stay in control. "I've told you before that I appreciate that you're trying to help me, but this is ridiculous! There's nothing wrong with the way I've been playing this scene. I think you just want to criticize me."

"Now aren't we being a little sensitive?" Dean said, raising an eyebrow. "I think that I, of all people, know how *Romeo and Juliet* should be played. If you can't accept professional advice, then you don't belong in a professional production."

"*I* don't belong?" Joanna said. Her mouth hung open in disbelief. Then she drew in a breath and said calmly, "I think the scene is fine as it is."

"But this scene is extremely important—" Dean began.

"Dean, Dean—Joanna is right," Josh Forster interrupted. "That exchange was fine," he said calmly. "We don't have much time left, so we need to move on. Now, what really needs work is your fighting scene in Act Three."

"What? My fight scene?" Dean exclaimed. He looked at Josh indignantly. "Well, I'd like to know who suddenly made *you* the director."

Nancy stood off to the side, watching the scene with fascination. Dean Batlan was definitely someone to watch, she thought.

Josh adjusted his glasses and said in a superior tone, "Well, if you'd like to talk about credentials, that's fine. I may not be the director, but I think all my years of study and research in London speak for themselves. And when I tell you that the way you're using a rapier is wrong, believe me, it's wrong. I happen to be a student of fencing, as well."

"Well . . . well!" Dean Batlan managed to sputter.

With that Josh got up and picked up the rapier. Flourishing the long, light, sword, he began demonstrating various movements and thrusts.

"Now, remember," he said to Dean, "when

you go to stab Tybalt, your enemy, the lunge has to be placed—"

"Oh, this is really too much!" Dean exploded. "I'm being treated like a child. I don't care what kind of so-called expert you're supposed to be. I'll play the role as I see fit."

"But, Dean, Josh has some really good ideas," said Joanna, who had been watching them from the side. "I think you ought to listen to him," she added.

"I think I'll do exactly as I please!" Dean retorted.

"You're completely unreasonable," Josh put in.

"That's enough!" a voice called. "Let's stop all of this bickering and get ready." Nancy turned to see Schotter approaching the stage. "The audience is starting to arrive. Let's go!"

Nancy slipped out of the tent. She had learned at least one thing—Dean Batlan seemed to be very angry and pompous. Dean acted like someone who wasn't getting the money and respect he thought he deserved.

Hurrying back toward the pavilion, Nancy found Queen Elizabeth's procession being formed. The queen was to be the guest of honor at every performance of *Romeo and Juliet*. Nancy slid into line behind Bess, who was still flushed and excited from her dancing efforts. Nancy filled Bess in on the events at the last-minute rehearsal.

The girls watched as Martine DeVries was helped onto the litter to be carried in. The actress inserted an old-fashioned fan into a bejeweled fan holder. The holder was an antique case that held the triangular bottom of the fan. She popped open the fan for a dramatic effect.

One person after another, the procession entered through the back of the theater and walked down the aisle to the front row, which was reserved for the court. Nancy saw that Martine's usual scowl had been transformed into Queen Elizabeth's smooth, regal smile. Nancy also noticed the hushed solemnity of the audience. Everyone acted as if they were full of respect for the queen.

But in the next instant the quiet was shattered by a sharp cracking noise. Nancy spun around in time to see one of the rods that held the litter break in two. The litter lurched to the side, plunging Martine toward the ground!

Quickly the actors carrying the broken side of the seat grabbed the frame. But their actions came a moment too late. With nothing to hold her in, Martine DeVries came tumbling off the side!

4

An Unlucky Break

Nancy and Bess looked on helplessly as Martine landed in a heap on the ground. The audience gasped.

The queen's ladies-in-waiting and courtiers immediately gathered around her, including Nancy and Bess.

"Are you all right?" Bess asked anxiously.

Martine looked up in a daze. "I—I'm all right, I think," she said shakily. The hooped skirt of her heavily brocaded dress stuck out awkwardly to one side, while a bit of wire was poking out from the high collar. Her crown had been thrown off, and strands of hair hung over her face. A low buzz of voices filled the theater as the audience stared in astonishment.

Snapping back to attention, Martine held her arms out to those closest to her. "Help me up," she whispered fiercely.

"But are you sure you're okay?" one of the actors asked.

"I'm fine," she said impatiently under her breath. "Now get me up!"

As Martine was brought to her feet, the audience burst into applause. Though still a bit shaky, Martine gave the crowd a regal smile.

Turning to the ladies and gentlemen of her court, she said quietly, "Okay, let's just head down to our seats. And," she said, gesturing toward the broken litter, "get rid of that thing." She smoothed her hair back, put on her crown, and adjusted her dress.

The procession headed down to the reserved seats as the litter was quickly carried out of the theater by troupe members dressed as footmen. Martine took her seat in the middle of the front row, and the rest of the procession sat around her. As they sat down, Nancy was deep in thought, wondering how the litter could have broken.

Suddenly Martine grabbed the sides of her seat. "My fan!" she exclaimed, looking about her. "Where's my fan?"

Immediately, Nancy, Bess, and the other ladies of the court began looking for the fan she'd been carrying.

"I must have dropped it when I fell," Martine said. She nudged a courtier sitting next to her.

"Go see if you can find it before the play starts. Hurry!"

A few minutes later the actor came back, shaking his head. "Sorry. I don't see it anywhere," he said.

"Oh, great," Martine said irritably. "It's not enough that I'm thrown to the ground. Now someone steals my fan, too."

Nancy leaned toward Bess. "I think we should go check out that broken litter," she whispered. "I heard someone say it was at the storage shed."

"Now?" Bess said. "The play's starting."

Nancy nodded. "We can watch the play tomorrow night," she whispered. The two girls got up and left the theater.

On their way to the storage shed, they met up with George. "I saw the whole thing from offstage," she said. "Martine's a real trooper. It's lucky she wasn't seriously hurt. Aren't you going to watch the play?"

"Not tonight," Nancy said. She explained her plan, and George decided to join them. As the three girls entered the storage shed, the troupe members who'd been carrying the litter were just leaving.

"Poor Martine!" Bess said. "I think I'd be a little angry, too, if I got dumped to the ground in front of a theater full of people."

"I think she's probably more than a little

angry," Nancy said. She began to inspect the red cushioned seat, covered in an antique floral pattern. Suddenly she saw a piece of paper lodged in the seat. She grabbed it, unfolded it, and raised her eyebrows. "Uh-oh," she said. "Looks like our note writer is back. Same old-fashioned writing as the first." She began to read to Bess and George.

"What wilt thou do? Thou wilt not murder me?
Help, ho!"
The queen was wise to be afraid of Hamlet
Even though her final hour hadn't come yet.
And you'd be wise to take care, too.
Because your final hour may be upon you!

"I don't like this at all," Bess said, her eyes wide with fright.

"I don't, either," George admitted. "That note is almost a death threat."

Nancy nodded. "It's a pretty forceful warning, all right." She scowled at the piece of paper. "The lines quoted here are spoken by the queen in *Hamlet*. Since Martine is the queen, and she's the only one who rides the litter, this threat must be aimed at her."

Nancy paused. "But who would want to harm Martine? And why? She wasn't the target of that falling weapons rack or the first note."

32

"It's like trying to figure out a riddle," George observed.

"A pretty gruesome riddle," Bess added.

"Well, no matter who the target is, the note seems to indicate that the litter breaking was no accident," Nancy said. She bent down to examine the broken pole. It had snapped near the back end, just in front of where the rear footman gripped it. The end was smoothly split about three-quarters of the way through.

"This wood doesn't look as if it splintered under pressure," she said. "It looks as though this rod has been sawed partway through."

George bent down next to her. "So someone cut through the wood just enough to make it easier to break."

Nancy nodded. "As soon as enough pressure was put on the piece, it was bound to break." She thought for a moment. "George, do you know who has access to this storage shed?"

George shrugged. "As far as I know, just about everybody in the festival."

At Nancy's suggestion the girls searched through the shed for clues, but besides a few pieces of trash, the shed was empty. "We might as well go back to the theater," Nancy said with a sigh. "I'd like to talk to Philip Schotter."

As the girls approached the theater, they saw spectators milling about the refreshment stands.

"This must be intermission time," Nancy said. "Let's go backstage and find Philip."

The girls found the director congratulating actors on their performances and giving directions for the next scene. Suddenly loud, quick steps were heard coming across the backstage area. Nancy turned to see Martine DeVries heading toward Schotter.

Schotter exclaimed, "Martine! Thank goodness you're all right. How on earth could that litter have broken?"

Martine stared at him coldly. "As if you didn't know," she said in a biting voice. "You've been waiting to see me fall on my face, haven't you? You want me to make a fool of myself, right?"

"What are you talking about?" Schotter said, sounding surprised. "I don't know what happened with the litter. But we'll find out and—"

But Martine was no longer listening. Pushing her way through the crowd of actors, she marched up to J.Z. "And *you*," she continued in her bitter tone. "Your shoddy props could have killed me."

J.Z. immediately began to protest. "Look, I'm real sorry this happened," he said, holding up his hands. "I promise you, Martine, that litter was thoroughly checked this afternoon."

"He's right," George said, rushing to his defense. "We looked it over when we cleaned it, and it was fine."

34

Martine turned her deadly stare to George. "Who on earth are *you?*" she said. Seeing George's volunteer badge only made her angrier. "Do you actually think I'd trust one of you volunteers?" she asked. "Maybe it was you who stole my fan and fan holder." With that, she marched offstage.

"Whew!" Bess exclaimed. "Gracious queen becomes ice queen."

J.Z. shook his head. "I respect Martine a lot as an actress," he said. "She's a real pro. But that temper of hers . . ." He trailed off with a long whistle. "Anyway, thanks for backing me up, George. And thanks for all your help today," he added, before turning away.

"Martine sure makes it hard for anyone to feel sorry for her," Nancy said to Bess and George. "But I still don't think that would make someone want to actually harm her. And that note sounded pretty threatening."

"Well, at least we know one thing about the person writing these notes," Bess said.

"What's that?" Nancy said with interest.

"He or she must know Shakespeare," Bess said.

"Great," George replied. "That narrows it down to just about everybody here."

Nancy began to look around for Schotter again. She wanted to tell him about the latest note before the play started again. Finally she spotted him in a corner of the backstage area. He was

35

talking to a man in a business suit with his back to Nancy. The two seemed to be deep in conversation.

The man in the suit turned slightly, and Nancy caught a glimpse of his face. She immediately recognized him as Louis Romero, a local businessman. Handsome and dark-haired, Romero was becoming well known in River Heights as a flamboyant and ambitious business promoter and developer. Nancy was surprised to see him at the Elizabethan festival. She hadn't known he was interested in local arts.

Moving casually toward the two men, Nancy came close enough to hear their conversation. Schotter's voice rose to an angry pitch.

"Look, I don't know how many ways I can say no," he said. "Our festival has been well received in River Heights for three years. I have absolutely no interest in changing it."

"Phil, I've been a patient man," Romero responded smoothly. "But you're making this difficult. I don't have to tell you again that my fair would be a great business opportunity for you."

"You don't have to say one more word about your medieval fair," Schotter said, gritting his teeth. "I'm not sharing our pavilion space next year. River Heights doesn't want your fair, and I don't want any so-called partners. You'll have to make other arrangements."

"You're crazy!" Romero shouted. "With my

high-budget, high-tech fair here to pull people in, your rinky-dink, one-week sideshow could finally start counting on some serious profits."

"I said no," Schotter said, trying to control his anger. "And that's my final word."

"That's too bad, Phil," Romero said, losing his cool. He pointed a finger at Schotter. "But with or without your cooperation, my festival is in—so I guess yours is going to be out!"

5

Her Majesty's Secret Service

As Nancy watched Romero stomp off stage, new questions came to her mind. Apparently, Romero wanted to develop another festival in River Heights, a medieval fair. And if he needed to share pavilion space with the Elizabethan festival, then he must want the fair to be at the same time as the festival. But Schotter was obviously not interested in sharing his spot with Romero's flashier production. So, Nancy wondered, how far would Romero go to get the pavilion space? Would he be willing to sabotage the festival?

As Schotter walked across the backstage area, Nancy approached him. She told the director about the second note. "I don't get it," Schotter said, sighing. "And I'm not sure I have the energy to think about this now. The next scene's about to start. But I do appreciate all your help so far, Nancy. Let's try to talk tomorrow." Nancy nodded in understanding. The festival director looked worn out.

It was already past nine o'clock when Nancy left Bess's house, where she had eaten dinner with the two cousins. George was staying there for the week while her parents were out of town. Over BLT sandwiches, Nancy had given them a brief account of Louis Romero's appearance. As she drove toward her own house, she reviewed the mysterious events of the day, focusing on the two threatening notes. Leaving notes was pretty bold, she thought. The note writer had obviously spent a lot of time on the wording. And it took someone who had access to the trailers and props.

There were so many possibilities, it was frustrating. Nancy wasn't even sure who, if anyone, was the target of the notes, or why. Martine seemed to be one of the direct targets. But the weapons rack could have fallen on anyone. So how were the two incidents connected? she wondered.

Romero's threat to Philip Schotter was still ringing in her mind, too. Perhaps the acts of vandalism were his first attempts to drive the Elizabethan festival out of town. They were certainly scaring the members of the troupe. And, like any other spectator, Romero had access to the storage facilities.

Nancy recalled Dean Batlan's threat to Josh about "bringing the show down." Dean seemed to feel he deserved better treatment and, perhaps, more money. Maybe he was directing his anger at the festival, she thought.

As she pulled into her driveway, Nancy remembered Bess's words of warning that morning about not getting involved in another mystery. I guess it's too late for that now, she thought, smiling.

The next morning Nancy pulled her blue Mustang into the festival grounds a few minutes before noon. She felt refreshed after a good night's sleep. She headed for the costume trailer, where she had planned to meet Bess and George, who'd driven over in Bess's car.

Bess was just leaving the trailer when Nancy arrived. "Hi, there!" Bess said cheerfully. She was already in costume, wearing the green dress of the day before. But today she also had her hair pulled up under an elaborate hat. "George had to head backstage already," Bess explained. "I'm going to watch some of the afternoon games. Should I wait for you?"

Nancy shook her head. "Go ahead. I'll catch up with you later."

After quickly changing into her ivory-colored dress, Nancy headed toward the town square.

The afternoon was warm and sunny, and spectators were spilling into the festival grounds. Musicians, jugglers, and clowns strolled through the square, filling the air with excitement.

Three sides of the square were made up of false sixteenth-century building fronts. The fourth side remained open, so visitors could enter the square. A grassy area was in the middle.

On a lawn outside the square Nancy came upon a group of men playing a sixteenth-century game called bowls. She thought it looked like a combination of bowling and horseshoes. The men took turns rolling balls toward a single ball set as a mark some distance away. The object was to roll closest to the ball. A large group of spectators had gathered to watch, some taking turns themselves.

Nancy walked up to another area where several men in costume were demonstrating firearms. While an audience watched from a safe distance, they showed how to load gunpowder and bullets. Once the bullets and gunpowder were packed in, a lighted match was held to loose gunpowder. It looked to Nancy like a slow, dangerous process.

After strolling through the festival a bit longer, Nancy headed for Philip Schotter's office. She hoped he might know something about Dean Batlan or Louis Romero that could help her.

Approaching Schotter's trailer, she noticed that the door was slightly open. Hoping this was a sign that the director was there, she reached up to knock—but she suddenly stopped. A woman's low throaty voice could be heard inside the trailer.

Nancy immediately recognized the voice as Martine DeVries's. At first she thought Martine was talking to Schotter, but when Nancy didn't hear Schotter's voice, she realized that Martine was speaking on the telephone.

Quietly positioned outside the door, Nancy heard the actress say, "No, darling, I don't have any real evidence yet. But I'd have to be a fool not to see what's going on here."

Darling? Martine must be talking to her husband, Nancy thought.

After a short pause Martine resumed speaking. "Well, it's obvious. I'm being treated like yesterday's news. Schotter must think I'm not much of an attraction for the festival anymore, so he's going to replace me. But I have a little surprise for him."

Nancy's heart skipped a beat.

"No, of course he didn't *say* he was going to fire me," Martine said irritably. Nancy smiled. The person on the other end of the phone must have asked the same question she had been thinking.

Lowering her voice, Martine continued. "I think Schotter's been secretly looking for someone to replace me. He'll just wait for the right opportunity, and then he'll quietly fire me.

"I'll tell you something, though," Martine said after a pause, her voice colder than before. "He won't get rid of me so easily. Maybe he's forgotten about my contract, but he has to keep me to the end! Listen, darling, I have to be going."

Nancy quietly hurried around to the back of the trailer. As soon as she heard a door slam, she peeked around the corner to see Martine walking down the row of trailers.

Nancy let out her breath. She understood now why Martine had seemed so angry at Schotter after the play the night before. She believed that Schotter wanted her out of the festival so badly that he tampered with the litter.

But that doesn't seem right, Nancy thought as her breathing became more even. Schotter had seemed pleased that Martine, who had many years of stage acting to her credit, was part of the festival. But maybe Schotter didn't really feel that way, maybe he was an even better actor than Martine. Perhaps Martine, in her anger at being replaced, was the one creating the disturbances at the festival.

Nancy warned herself against jumping to conclusions. Martine's anger about her contract might lead her to take action against the festival, but Nancy had no proof of that. And how would that explain the falling weapons rack? Still, Nancy decided to keep her eye on Martine. And she resolved to try to speak to Schotter about Martine's contract.

"Do you really think Schotter wants to replace her?" Bess asked when Nancy filled her in on Martine's telephone conversation. The two friends were seated at a banquet table for the queen's feast.

"I don't know," Nancy said thoughtfully. "If he does, I haven't seen any indication of it."

As it was already late afternoon, Nancy suggested that they walk over to the theater, to meet up with the procession. They didn't want to miss the performance of *Romeo and Juliet*, especially since they had missed it the previous evening.

A few moments later they were part of the queen's procession headed toward the front row of the theater. The litter had been repaired, but Martine looked nervous as she was carried down the aisle. To everyone's relief, she was delivered to her seat without harm. Nancy and Bess took their seats to await the start of the play. Before the lights went out, Nancy was surprised to see Louis Romero sitting a few rows away. His tanned face was set in a permanent scowl. She wondered what he hoped to gain by watching the play.

The play began and immediately drew the

audience into the story of the feuding families, the Capulets and Montagues. The sword fight in the first scene was very well done, and Nancy found herself absorbed in the drama.

When Dean Batlan entered the stage, as the lovesick Romeo, his booming voice and dramatic presence immediately commanded attention.

Bess leaned over to Nancy. "I'm no theater critic," she whispered, "but doesn't he seem to be overplaying the role a bit?"

Nancy nodded in agreement. But the audience seemed to enjoy it. At the end of Act One, after Romeo and Juliet's first scene together, applause filled the theater.

As the second scene in Act Two began, Nancy and Bess exchanged smiles. They recognized it as the famous balcony scene. From the ground Romeo spoke to Juliet as she stood outside her bedroom on a balcony. The stage was decorated to look like an orchard. To the right, a large wooden prop, painted to look like the side of Juliet's house, had been rolled out. There was an actual balcony on top, along with French doors that opened out to it. Although the stage was about level with Nancy, the balcony looked to be at least ten feet high.

Nancy could see Joanna Messerman, as Juliet, hovering behind the thinly curtained doors, waiting for Romeo to finish his opening speech.

Finally she stepped out to the balcony, and putting her hand on the railing, she began, "O Romeo, Romeo, wherefore art thou Romeo?"

But just as she finished the line, the balcony railing gave way from under her. In the next instant Juliet toppled from the balcony toward the stage!

6

Poetry in Motion

The audience gasped in horror as Joanna Messerman fell toward the stage floor. Dean Batlan instinctively threw out his arms to catch her. He tried to stop her fall, but the force of the impact brought him to his knees. There was a loud thud followed by momentary silence. Joanna, lying partly on Dean and partly on the stage, slowly lifted her head. Her face wore a shocked expression.

Dean, still on his knees, helped her to a sitting position. "Are you all right?" he asked quietly. Joanna nodded, looking stunned.

In the meantime the actors in the previous scene had run onstage to assist Joanna and Dean. They helped the two actors to their feet and pulled the railing backstage. Standing up, Dean and Joanna realized that the audience was watching their every move.

Schotter stood anxiously in the wings, motioning for them to exit the stage.

Instead, Joanna turned to Dean and took his hands. "Oh, Romeo," she said in a melodramatic voice. "It is no secret anymore. I have really fallen for you!"

Dean looked at her in surprise, then smiled. "Juliet, my love, you are truly an angel come down from heaven."

The audience burst into laughter and gave the two actors an enthusiastic round of applause.

"I'm so glad they're not hurt," Bess said to Nancy, her hands clasped tightly. "What a terrible fall!"

Nancy nodded grimly as she continued clapping. "They sure made a professional recovery, though," she said to Bess. "I guess the show really must go on."

As the applause subsided, Dean and Joanna smoothly picked up the scene from where they had left off before the fall. But now there was no balcony.

Although Nancy was impressed by the actors' recovery, she couldn't concentrate on the scene. All she could think about was the balcony. As the scene came to an end, she nudged Bess. "I'm going to run backstage," she whispered. Slipping quietly from her seat, she moved quickly across the front row and around the side of the stage.

Soon the balcony scene was over, and the props

crew brought the balcony backstage and began to set up a new backdrop in its place for the next scene. Dean and Joanna entered the backstage tent and were immediately surrounded by the concerned cast and troupe members.

Dean was furious. "Can someone tell me what in heaven is going on here?" he said to no one in particular. "These second-rate props will kill us all! It was only my—uh, our—professionalism that saved that scene from disaster. I've probably permanently injured my knees! I—"

Schotter interrupted him. "Dean, I'm sorry, but we haven't time. You're in the next scene."

"I'm aware of that!" Dean bellowed, turning away abruptly.

Nancy saw Joanna Messerman as she practically fell into a chair. Though she had bravely finished the scene, it was obvious that her fall had weakened her. "I think I just need to rest before my next scene," she said to those standing around her. "My ankle is a little sore."

"Should I call a doctor?" Schotter asked in a worried voice.

"Oh, no," Joanna said. "It's nothing serious. I've sprained my ankle before, and it hurt much worse than this. Just give me a few minutes, okay?"

Nancy turned to check out the balcony, which the props crew had rolled backstage. J.Z. was already at work, repairing the railing. George, who was standing near him, looked up as Nancy approached.

"That was a close one, huh?" George said.

"A little too close," Nancy responded, frowning. "What happened?"

Before George could answer, J.Z. angrily said, "Somebody's been messing with the props, that's what happened. The screws holding the railing to the balcony had all been loosened. As soon as that poor girl leaned against it, the railing was sure to go." He paused for a moment. "You have to be pretty sick to do something like this," he muttered, going back to work.

Nancy walked around to the back of the wooden structure. There she noticed a set of stairs leading up to the French doors that opened to the small balcony, where Joanna had been standing.

Nancy walked up the stairs and stood at the glass doors, looking through the almost transparent curtains. Looking up and down, Nancy spotted what she thought was a fold in the curtain. Reaching up to smooth it, her hand closed on a piece of paper pinned to the curtain.

"Uh-oh," George said, watching from below. "I'll bet I can guess what that is."

Nancy unpinned the note and unfolded it as she came down the stairs. Sure enough, it was another note written in the familiar old-fashioned printing:

"O Romeo, Romeo, wherefore art thou Romeo?"
Look out from the balcony and oh! what a
    view:
The spectators think this show is through.
They're right, you know, for I'll bring you
    all down
It's time to move to a new town.

"Not exactly Shakespeare, is it?" George commented.

"I don't think the writer is too concerned with the poetry," Nancy said. She hesitated for a moment, and then said, "George, do you think J.Z. could have had anything to do with any of this?"

George shook her head firmly. "He's about the hardest worker in the troupe," she said. "And he's very loyal to Schotter. Besides, I was with him all afternoon, and he didn't go near the balcony."

Nancy nodded, still frowning. "Just about anyone could have had access to the balcony, right, George?"

George nodded. "As far as I know, this tent is open. People run in and out all day."

"So someone could have loosened the screws earlier this afternoon," Nancy said. "And no one would have bothered to check the balcony, since it was fine last night."

"But why would anyone want to hurt Joanna?"

George said. "She's the only one who uses the balcony, and she seems pretty popular around here."

Nancy looked at the note again. "I have a feeling our mystery poet is choosing his or her words very carefully here," she said. She read from the note: " 'I'll bring you all down.' I don't think he or she is trying to hurt a specific person. He or she wants to hurt the whole show."

"So I guess this note writer just doesn't care if an innocent person happens to get hurt in the process," George said angrily. "It's so frustrating! And why would someone want to hurt the festival, anyway?"

"Maybe because that someone is afraid of getting fired," Nancy mused. She filled George in on Martine's telephone conversation.

"Martine does seem like the kind of person who wouldn't go down without a fight," George remarked.

"But she's not the only person who has a problem with the festival," Nancy said. She reminded George of Louis Romero's plan to start another festival. "And I can't stop thinking about Dean Batlan's complaints about the way the festival is run."

"And don't forget—he thinks he deserves more money, and he hasn't been too happy about that," George said. "Come to think of it, he did some quick thinking to catch Joanna. Maybe he knew the balcony was about to break."

The two girls looked up to see Josh Forster, the consultant, walking toward them. "Good evening, Miss Drew," he said politely. He nodded at George and adjusted his wire-rimmed glasses. "I see our poet is back," he said, raising his eyebrows as he spotted the note in Nancy's hand. "What does *this* verse say?"

Nancy shrugged. "Not much. Someone is threatening the festival again. I don't know who it is yet," she admitted, "but I'm working on it."

"What happened tonight was just terrible," Josh said, shaking his head. "I'd hate to think that someone could be seriously injured. Do be careful yourself, Miss Drew." Then he added in his reserved manner, "Philip Schotter wants to meet with all volunteers after the play."

"Tonight's stage accident was pretty scary," Schotter began when he had everybody together. "And we intend to find out who's responsible for it," he added, looking at Nancy. "In fact, I'm on my way to Joanna's trailer to make sure she's okay. But I'd also like to make sure that our festival gets some positive publicity, despite these accidents. So . . ." He paused. "I'm asking those of you from River Heights to wear your costumes home tonight."

"What?" one young man said in surprise. He was dressed in short pants and tights. Other volunteers looked at one another with raised eyebrows.

The director grinned. "We've found that this is a great way to get people interested in the festival," he said. "If you wear your costumes when you go grocery shopping, stop at a gas station, or ride public transportation, you might get strange looks—but you'll also have people asking you questions. Then you can tell them about the festival."

"How about if I wear this dress to my aerobics class tomorrow morning?" one of the ladies-in-waiting asked Schotter. The other volunteers laughed.

"Attendance has been quite good at the festival this year. And I think with your help, we can keep it that way," Schotter said. "Just check out your costume with Donna Vasquez before you leave tonight. That way we'll be able to keep track of who takes what."

When the group broke up, Nancy turned to Bess and George. "I think I'll head straight home," she said. "I'll see you two tomorrow."

"Aren't you coming with us?" Bess asked.

"Coming where?" George asked her cousin. "I thought we were going home, too."

"Weren't you listening?" Bess said, smiling. "We're supposed to be seen around town in our

54

costumes. I think we should start by getting some frozen yogurt."

Nancy laughed. "Sounds good to me," she said. "Let's meet at the yogurt place near my house."

George looked at Nancy and Bess in their long, full Elizabethan dresses and then looked down at her own jeans and T-shirt. "Okay," she said with a sigh, "but can we find a frozen yogurt place that has a drive-through window?"

Bess grabbed her cousin's arm. "Come on," she said. "We'll meet you there, Nan."

About fifteen minutes later the three girls made their way into the frozen yogurt shop. A few customers were placing their orders at the counter, while others were already eating ice cream at tables.

Nancy and Bess led the way to the counter, the full skirts of their dresses swaying back and forth. Behind her, Nancy heard a small boy's voice say, "Mommy, look at those funny ladies."

"Shhh! It's not polite to point," his mother said.

George ducked her head in embarrassment as she went up to the counter. "Can we get this to go?" she muttered to Nancy and Bess. "Everyone here is staring at us."

The teenage girl at the counter laughed as she turned to wait on the girls. "What can I get for you?" she said in a friendly voice.

"A mask," George said.

Ignoring her cousin, Bess said, "I'll have a chocolate and vanilla swirl in a cup, with granola on top."

"Is that for here, or will you be taking it back to the castle?" the girl said with a grin.

Bess and Nancy laughed. "We've just come from the Elizabethan festival at the pavilion," Nancy explained. "It's going on all this week. We're volunteers."

"Oh, yeah, I heard about that," the young girl said. "We have fliers announcing it here at the counter. In fact, that family over there was just asking about it." She pointed toward the windows.

The girls looked over at a family of four seated at a nearby table. "Why don't we go sit next to them, so we can talk to them about the festival?" Bess suggested.

"Oh, great," George said. "Why don't the two of you act out a scene from *Romeo and Juliet* while you're at it?"

"Not a bad idea," Bess said, winking at Nancy.

George shook her head. "This could be a long evening," she said with a sigh.

When Nancy arrived at Bess's house the next morning, only Bess got into the car.

"Where's George?" Nancy asked. "I hope she's not too embarrassed to be seen with us anymore, after last night."

Bess laughed. "I think she survived—after all, we didn't do any acting. Actually, George had to leave for the festival early today. J.Z. had asked her to help out with a weapons demonstration that begins exactly at twelve."

"What does she have to do?" Nancy asked.

"She's supposed to help at a fencing match. She's going to be dressed as a nobleman, I think," she said, smiling.

As soon as they reached the festival, Nancy and Bess headed over to the center of the town square. The grassy area in the center had been roped off. A small crowd of spectators was gathered around two people in costume. Nancy and Bess made their way to the front.

George and another troupe member stood in front of the group on a slightly raised platform. Nancy and Bess smiled when they saw George in a fake beard and mustache and a fancy hat cocked to one side.

The person next to George explained that the fencing match would be a re-creation of the fight in *Hamlet* between Hamlet and Laertes. "The two characters meet in the last scene of the play in what proves to be a fatal fencing match," he said. "Of course," he added with a smile, "we aren't taking any chances here. Our actors will be using fake swords."

With that, two men stepped up on the platform, and George handed them each thin swords.

"This is called a rapier," she said to the spectators. Then she stepped off the platform.

From her place in the front row, Nancy had a good view of the two demonstrators, who separated and faced each other. They lifted their rapiers and slowly began circling each other, waiting for a moment to attack.

Suddenly the taller man thrust his rapier at the other. The point of the rapier hit the smaller man's upper arm. Several "oohs" could be heard from the spectators as the smaller man leapt back, holding his arm.

"It's a good thing those weapons are fakes," Bess whispered to Nancy. Nancy nodded absently, her eyes riveted on the smaller actor, who was now getting into position to return the hit. Then she let out a little gasp.

"Bess," she said quickly, "there's blood on that man's arm!"

7

Courtly Clues

Before Bess had time to react, Nancy ran in between the two demonstrators, who had continued their swordplay. The men pulled back their rapiers in surprise. "Your arm," Nancy said to the smaller one, pointing to his upper arm. "It's bleeding!"

The man looked down in shock. A red stain was spreading across his white shirtsleeve. Pulling the wet cloth away from his skin, he blurted out, "Hey! What's going on? I thought these things were fakes!"

George jumped up to the platform to join Nancy and the two swordsmen. By now a general buzz was arising from the audience as they moved in closer to see what had happened.

"Let me see your rapiers again," George said quietly to the two demonstrators. Holding the two swords, George looked at them carefully for a moment, and then turned to the actor in charge, who had just jumped down from the platform. "These rapiers are real," she said grimly.

"Real?" he exclaimed. Gasps were heard from the crowd, and the man lowered his voice. "How can that be? We brought the fake ones over here this morning."

"I don't know," George said. "But I think we better do something about it—now. Let's get you to the first-aid station," she said to the smaller swordsman, who was applying pressure to the cut on his upper arm. "And let's figure out what happened to the fake swords," she added. She and the actor set off toward the first-aid station, located in one of the rows of trailers.

As the audience continued to murmur, the actor in charge of the demonstration stepped forward with a nervous smile. "Uh, folks, there's just been a little mix-up here. If you'll be patient, we'll, uh . . . we'll . . ." He trailed off, looking about him in confusion.

Suddenly he spotted one of the festival's jugglers. Grabbing the unsuspecting juggler, the actor pulled the man up to the platform. "How about some juggling, folks?" he said, trying to sound excited. "Look who just popped in— Jerome, our court juggler!" Jerome looked rather confused, but after a nudge from the actor in charge, he began to juggle.

While the spectators focused their attention on the juggler, Nancy made her way to the side of

60

the platform. A small table had been placed to the side of the raised wooden area. On top of it were two goblets of water for the fencing opponents. Looking down at the goblets, Nancy noticed a corner of white paper peeking out from under one of them. She felt her heart sink a little. Here we go again, she thought, pulling the paper out. She unfolded and read:

"To be, or not to be,"
There's really no question
For as you can see
I decide if you will be.

"Oh, no! Not another one!" exclaimed a voice next to Nancy. Nancy turned to see Bess standing beside her.

"What's going on?" Bess said, her eyes full of worry. "Is that actor going to be all right?"

Nancy reassured her friend that the man's wound didn't seem to be too deep. "But it looks as though somebody switched the fake rapiers for real ones," she said. Suddenly the two girls saw George walking briskly toward the demonstration area, accompanied by J.Z. Nancy and Bess ran to catch up with them.

Nancy showed George and J.Z. the note she had found under the goblet. "Whoever is writing these must be feeling pretty confident," she said. "This note is almost teasing us."

"I can't imagine what would have happened if those two actors had continued fighting," Bess said with a shudder.

"They shouldn't have gotten as far as they did," George said angrily. "I thought there was something strange about those rapiers when I picked them up from the ground and handed them to those two actors. They felt really heavy," she said. "This morning when we practiced, the fake rapiers J.Z. had given me were much lighter. I should have realized that these were the wrong ones." George shook her head in frustration.

"It's not your fault," J.Z. said. "How are you supposed to know that somebody would be crazy enough to switch the swords? And the fake swords look quite real—the only difference is the dull blades and the lighter weight."

"Are you sure the fake ones were brought to the demonstration area this morning?" Nancy asked George.

"Oh, yes," George said. "In fact, we set the table up and brought the rapiers over just a short time before the demonstration began. Somebody had to have switched them when I went back to the trailer to put my costume on."

"Where did the real rapiers come from?" Nancy asked.

"Now, that's what I don't get," J.Z. put in. "After that weapons rack fell down on Sunday, George, a few other crew members, and I moved all the real weapons into Phil Schotter's trailer. We were worried about people getting hurt, so we figured the closet in his trailer would be a pretty safe place."

Nancy frowned in concentration. "And who has access to that trailer?" she asked.

J.Z. thought for a moment. "Well, Phil has a phone hookup in there, so he usually keeps the door open to let the cast and crew use the phone," he answered. "But the closet is kept locked. I thought Phil was the only one with a key."

As J.Z. talked, Nancy remembered that Martine DeVries had used Schotter's trailer to make the phone call she had overheard. She wondered if Martine had managed to get into the closet. Nancy hadn't seen the actress yet that day.

"I'd like to take a look around the trailers," Nancy said. "Anybody want to join me?"

"Sorry," George said. "I should help clean up when this juggler is finished. I'll catch up with you later." She and J.Z. turned back to watch Jerome the juggler.

"I'll go," Bess said. "I think I've seen enough fencing for one day." She and Nancy headed toward the trailers, their full skirts swaying behind them.

"What are you going to look for, Nan?" Bess asked as they walked.

"I'm not really sure," Nancy admitted. "But

whoever exchanged those rapiers had to do it recently and quickly. Maybe he or she is still around or left some clue."

Bess looked alarmed. "We're not going to go poking through Schotter's trailer, are we? What if he comes back?"

Nancy shook her head. "I don't think our note writer would be anywhere near that trailer now. That would be too risky."

When they reached the costume trailer, Nancy saw a smaller trailer that she hadn't seen before.

The girls went up to the trailer and tried to open the door. It was locked.

"Maybe this is someone's personal trailer," Bess said nervously. "I don't think we should go in."

"I don't think it belongs to anyone," Nancy said, looking through a small window in the side of the trailer. "It looks like some kind of storage trailer. Maybe the door is just stuck."

"I think that's called being locked," Bess said doubtfully.

Nancy made a wry face at her friend and then quickly unpinned the volunteer badge from her dress. Its plastic covering made it just about the size of a credit card. Sliding the plastic badge into the opening between the door and the frame, she managed to push the locking lever back to the unlock position. When she pulled the handle again, the door opened easily.

"See?" Nancy said with a smile. "It was just a little stuck."

Inside the trailer, Nancy and Bess found themselves looking at piles of odds and ends—Elizabethan hats, shoes, goblets, buckles, and stockings. Boxes and trunks were piled on the floor, and clothing and accessories were scattered on top of them. "I guess these are just extras," Nancy said as she and Bess began poking through the piles.

"Oooh, look at this," Bess said, throwing a long velvet cape over her shoulders. Both girls had a sneezing fit as the cape kicked up a cloud of dust.

Near the back of the trailer was a large trunk. Kneeling down, Nancy lifted the lid to find a man's costume that appeared to have been carelessly tossed inside. She sifted through articles of clothing until her hand hit the bottom of the trunk, making a hollow tapping noise. She hit the bottom in several places and heard the same hollow sound.

"Is someone knocking?" Bess said, looking up from the pile she'd been browsing through.

"That's me," Nancy said. "Listen to this," she said, tapping some more. "This trunk must have a fake bottom!" she said excitedly. She hurriedly pulled out all the clothes and ran her hand along the back edge of the bottom. A small tab stuck out in the middle of the edge. Grasping it with her fingers, she carefully pulled up. With a little effort the bottom lifted out. Nancy found herself looking at a small metal box on the true bottom of the trunk.

Bess peered over Nancy's bent form as Nancy lifted out a gray box. "What's that?" Bess asked, looking at the box, which was about the size of a shoe box.

"Let's take a look," Nancy said, opening the box.

"Ooo," Bess squealed, "more jewelry." The box was full of the same type of jeweled accessories they had seen in the costume trailer. Nancy and Bess began pulling out antique earrings, pins, and even a fan holder like the one Martine had been using. "I wonder if this is the same fan holder Martine dropped at the play," Nancy said, picking up the bejeweled holder.

"And I wonder why these pieces are in this trailer, instead of being used for the festival," Bess said, holding up a pin with sapphire-blue stones in it. "They're beautiful."

Suddenly the door to the trailer was flung open. Nancy and Bess whirled around to see Martine DeVries step inside. When the actress caught sight of Nancy and Bess, she stopped abruptly.

"Just what do you think you're doing?" Martine asked fiercely. Before Nancy or Bess could answer, Martine saw the jewels and let out a little gasp. "My jewels!" she exclaimed. "I've been looking everywhere for these." She looked down at the open metal box Nancy was holding. "I'll take that box now, thank you," she said, holding out her hands.

Nancy looked at her in surprise. *Her* jewels? she thought to herself. Martine was taking this Queen Elizabeth role just a little too seriously. "I'm not sure I understand," Nancy told the actress slowly. "We just happened to find this box as we were rummaging through the trailer," she added in explanation.

Martine sighed impatiently. "Those are obviously some of the pieces that were donated to the festival," she said. "Certain pieces were to be set aside to be worn by the queen. But they just disappeared when the festival started. They must have been in here all along."

Stepping closer to Nancy, Martine bent over the metal box and pulled the elaborate fan holder out. The top part was shaped like an upside down triangle, to hold the fan, and was decorated with large ruby stones. Descending from the point of the triangle was a line of smaller rubies. "My fan holder!" the actress exclaimed. "Thank goodness it's here. I thought it had been stolen on opening night."

Nancy and Bess exchanged glances. They remembered how angry Martine had been when the fan had been lost during her fall from the litter.

Nancy's mind began racing. How could the fan holder have ended up in here, with all these other pieces? she wondered. No one had been able to find it after the fall. And yet now it was buried in a box under a panel in a trunk. That had to be more than a coincidence, she thought. Could someone have found it and returned it to the trunk?

"Are you sure it's the same fan holder?" Nancy asked Martine.

Martine gave Nancy a haughty look. "Of course I'm sure. There's only one. Besides, I recognize the placement of the rubies." She held out her hands again. "Now I'd like that box."

Seeing Nancy hesitate, Bess blurted out, "But, Martine, you can't possibly wear all these pieces at once. I mean, the emerald earrings here don't even match the fan holder and that sapphire brooch you're holding."

Martine looked sharply at Bess and then looked down at the jewels. "Well, I suppose, if you're going to make a fuss about it, I'll let you wear a few of these, too. But under no circumstances is anyone but *me* going to carry the fan holder." Clutching the fan holder and the sapphire brooch, Martine stomped out of the trailer.

Bess let out a breath. "Whew! Martine doesn't exactly spread happiness wherever she goes, does she?" She looked at the emerald earrings and a ring with a large ruby. "But I guess she did leave these others for us." Smiling, Bess put on the earrings and handed Nancy the ruby ring. "See if the ring fits your finger, Nancy."

Absentmindedly, Nancy took the ring from Bess. It seemed to be quite a coincidence that Martine was hanging around the trailers just after the rapiers had been switched. Of course, Martine might have known about the storage trailer and been looking for a new costume piece. Still, she thought, there was something odd about the sudden appearance of both Martine and the missing fan holder in the trailer.

"I think we'd better go," Nancy said, slipping the ring on her finger. She lifted her hand up, admiring the ring. "Perfect fit," she said, smiling. She put the false bottom and the metal box back in the trunk and tossed the costumes back in on top of it. Then she and Bess left the trailer and hurried over to the other ladies of the court in the procession.

The third performance of *Romeo and Juliet* went smoothly, and Nancy and Bess enjoyed their first uninterrupted play since the festival began. Schotter reminded everyone that the next day, Wednesday, was a day off, but that if volunteers wanted to come help out with various projects, they could.

It was late evening when Nancy dropped Bess off. On her way home Nancy stopped at a gas station to fill her tank. When she got out of her car, she suddenly felt a sense of uneasiness—as if she were being watched. She unlatched the gas pump and looked around the station. A couple of other drivers were filling their tanks, too. The drivers, two older men, seemed to be completely absorbed in handling the gas hoses.

Nancy looked down at her own hose and caught sight of the full-skirted bottom of her Elizabethan dress. She smiled. She had forgotten that she was still in costume. I'll bet someone *was* looking at me, she thought. It's not too often that a sixteenth-century lady of the court pumps gas.

Arriving home, Nancy saw that Hannah had left a sandwich for her. Hannah Gruen had been the live-in housekeeper at the Drews' since Nancy's mother had died when Nancy was three. Nancy didn't know what she and her father, attorney Carson Drew, would do without her.

Hannah joined Nancy in the kitchen while Nancy ate her late supper. "Thanks for the sandwich," Nancy said. "I was so wrapped up in the play tonight that I almost forgot how hungry I was."

"How is the festival going?" Hannah asked. "*Romeo and Juliet* was always one of my favorites."

"The play went very well tonight," Nancy said. "Joanna Messerman, the actress who plays Juliet, got a standing ovation." Nancy went on to talk about the play. "Have you heard from Dad?" she asked Hannah. Carson Drew was out of town on business for the week.

"He called earlier to say hello. He says everything's going well, but he'll be glad to get home and get a good night's sleep," Hannah said.

"I think that's what I need, too," Nancy said wearily. Thanking Hannah again for the sandwich, Nancy said good night and headed up to bed.

After changing out of her Elizabethan dress and into pajamas, Nancy stretched out across the cool sheets. It wasn't long before she found herself drifting off to sleep, with images of the day's fencing match in her thoughts. She heard swords clashing against each other—one thud followed another dull thud . . . and then another one. Suddenly Nancy snapped awake. Swords don't thud when they hit each other, she thought.

She looked toward the window. A bit of light was coming in from the streetlight outside. Nancy propped herself up on her elbows. Focusing her eyes for a few seconds, she made out a shadow at her window.

Someone was trying to break into her bedroom!

8

A Visitor and a Visit

The shadowy figure was trying to lift Nancy's bedroom window. Quietly reaching for the telephone on her nightstand, Nancy dialed the number for the police department. In a low voice she gave her name and address and reported the break-in in progress.

Carefully hanging up the phone, Nancy kept her eyes glued to the window, hoping it was locked. She tried to map out her next move. She'd have to get out of her room and wake Hannah. Staying in the house could be dangerous. The would-be intruder might have a weapon.

A loud banging suddenly broke the tense silence. Someone was knocking on her bedroom door. "Nancy!" Hannah called. "Nancy! Are you awake?"

As Hannah's frightened cries rang through the bedroom, Nancy saw the shadow disappear from the window. She jumped out of bed and opened the door. Hannah stood in the hallway, clutching her bathrobe. "Oh, Nancy, I heard something—"

Nancy knew she had to hurry outside before the intruder got away. "Don't worry," she said, running past Hannah. "I've called the police."

Nancy threw a jacket on over her pajamas as she ran down the stairs. Bounding out the front door and across the front lawn, she headed toward the side of the house. There was a ladder propped against the side, leading up to her bedroom window. But there was nobody in sight.

Within the next couple of minutes two officers had arrived and began making a thorough search of the house and yard. They pulled the ladder down, and Nancy recognized it as her father's expanding aluminum model, which was usually kept in the garage. The officers looked for any unusual marks on the ladder, but found nothing. The lock on the garage door had evidently been picked, but nothing else in the garage was disturbed or missing.

Nancy met with Officer DelRio and her partner, Officer Wilkerson, in her living room a few moments later. She described hearing the thudding sounds and seeing the shadow in the window. As an afterthought, she mentioned her feeling that someone had been watching her at the gas station. Now she wondered if it had really been her costume someone had been looking at, after all.

The officers took down the information and told her they would call her if anything turned up. But they advised her not to be too hopeful—they didn't have much to go on.

After the officers had left, Nancy made a cup of hot chocolate for a worried Hannah. "Oh, Nancy, do you think someone has been watching the house?" Hannah asked. "Maybe someone knows your father is gone. Maybe we should call him," she said, her voice becoming more agitated.

"Now, Hannah, don't worry," Nancy said, squeezing the kindly housekeeper's hand. "Calling Dad would just worry him, and there's nothing he could do. We can tell him when he calls tomorrow. In the meantime," she said reassuringly, "the police have been alerted. And I have a feeling this intruder has been scared away from here for good."

Her words seemed to soothe Hannah a bit. But later, as Nancy was lying in bed, she found her words hadn't done much to relieve her own worries.

When Nancy awoke the next morning, she found it hard to believe that the bright sunshine was coming through the same window where she'd seen the dark shadow the night before.

She had slept later than usual, then showered and dressed at a leisurely pace. The fair was closed for the day, and Nancy didn't have to rush out. It felt good to put on jeans and a T-shirt after three days of wearing a bulky Elizabethan dress. She went outside and took a quick look around the house and yard to make sure she hadn't missed a clue the night before. But to her frustration, nothing turned up.

As she ate breakfast, Nancy decided to pay a visit to Louis Romero. She wanted to find out more about the businessman's plans for a medieval fair. It seemed suspiciously convenient that someone was trying to ruin the Elizabethan festival at the same time Romero wanted to gain support for his own fair.

After breakfast Nancy hopped in her car and headed toward Romero's office in downtown River Heights. It was located on the top floor of a large modern office building. After a quick elevator ride, Nancy pushed open a heavy glass door and found herself in a richly carpeted reception area.

Nancy politely explained to the receptionist that she hoped Mr. Romero could spare a few moments of his time to speak with her. Seeing the woman raise a skeptical eyebrow, Nancy quickly added that she worked as a free-lance writer. "I'm writing an article about the business climate in River Heights," she said smoothly. "It's an article I believe our local news magazine would like to publish."

The receptionist buzzed Romero's office. Lowering her voice, she briefly explained Nancy's story to Romero. A few moments later she hung up and turned to Nancy. "He says he can give you a few minutes," she said in a bored voice. "Down that hallway to the right. The big oak doors at the end."

Following the receptionist's instructions, Nancy found the double doors. As she reached out to knock, one of the doors flew open. Louis Romero stood in the doorway, a fixed smile plastered on his handsome face. "Miss Drew, isn't it?" he said, extending his hand. "Louis Romero. Aren't you Carson Drew's daughter?"

Nancy nodded as they shook hands. "I wasn't aware that you were working as a journalist," Romero said in his polished manner.

"I only work part-time, on a freelance basis," she said, following him into his office. Settling herself in a chair across from Romero's desk, she explained to him that she was asking prominent men and women in the business community about their current ventures. "For example, I've heard that you're promoting some kind of medieval fair."

Romero looked somewhat surprised, but quickly composed himself. "Why, yes," he said. "You know, I've always been a great supporter of our local arts. But I believe River Heights needs to start thinking big.

"Now, this medieval fair—that would be something people around here just haven't seen before. First, the whole thing takes place in a castle—not a real one, of course, but a great big replica, towers and the whole bit. Second, we won't make people sit through boring readings and exhibits."

He paused for emphasis. "Get this—we'll have rides. Real amusement park rides. You know, rides like Merlin's Magic Spin and King Arthur's Roller Coaster Express. Great, huh?"

"Sounds ambitious," Nancy said, smiling politely. She was glad Romero couldn't read her thoughts. Nancy didn't think Romero's fair had anything to do with medieval times.

"It *is* ambitious," Romero agreed enthusiastically. "And at this time next summer we could see it all happening. And I'll tell you something else, Nancy. The medieval fair could really be a shot in the arm for River Heights. Think of the revenue this thing could generate. People would flock from all over the state for this. And it would open up countless jobs for River Heights residents, as well."

"How long have you had an interest in the medieval period?" Nancy asked, looking up from the notebook in which she'd been pretending to take notes.

For a moment Romero looked confused. "Oh, I guess you could say I've always liked it." He hesitated. "But you know, I leave the historical stuff to the experts," he said with a wave of his hand. "I stick with what I know—how to bring people in and get them to spend their money," he said with a grin. He chuckled nervously. "Uh, that was a joke," he added.

"I got it," Nancy said without laughing. "Mr. Romero, where would the fair take place? Doesn't the annual Elizabethan festival reserve the pavilion space for this week every summer?" she asked.

Romero shifted uneasily in his seat. "Well," he said carefully, "my position is that the space could be shared. Just between you and me, the Elizabethan festival is a bit on the unprofessional side. But with an exciting main event, like my fair, the good people of River Heights will be given much more for their money."

"Couldn't the medieval fair come during a different week?" Nancy asked.

"No can do." Romero shook his head firmly. "We're talking about a major production here, one that's in demand across the country. I could reserve the fair only one week for next summer, and it's the same week that the Elizabethan thing is happening."

Nancy doubted that the medieval fair was that popular. She, for one, had never heard of it. "But what makes you think the festival will share its space?" Nancy asked. "It's been successful for the past three years, and many small businesses —such as local caterers and local arts groups— support the festival. It has a loyal following."

Romero sat up in his chair and narrowed his eyes at Nancy. "Those people will be loyal to anyone who can improve their business," he said coldly. "And frankly, I'm not so sure the festival will be able to hang on to their support this year, the way things are going now."

Nancy's heart began to beat a little faster. "What do you mean?" she asked as calmly as she could.

Romero's eyes narrowed even further. "Let's just say I've heard from reliable sources that this year's production has been marred by some unfortunate accidents. I think Philip Schotter's so-called Elizabethan festival might just die out."

"What makes you so sure of that?" Nancy asked.

Romero looked at her intently. "I guarantee you," he said. "It will die!"

9

On the Hunt

Nancy sat back in her chair in surprise. How could Romero guarantee that the Elizabethan festival would "die"? She wondered if he was simply speaking out of anger or if he could back up his words with actions. Was he the one writing the notes and vandalizing the festival?

Nancy didn't have time to continue her speculations. Romero seemed to be growing suspicious of her questioning. "I'm a very busy man, Miss Drew," he said, looking at his watch. "And I'm now behind schedule. You should be able to find your way out." Abruptly he grabbed some papers from his desk and swung his swivel chair away from Nancy.

Closing the notebook she had on her lap, Nancy politely thanked Romero and left the office.

Driving home, Nancy found herself thinking about Romero. Although he had tried to look cool and confident, his smooth surface had disappeared when Nancy began asking about the Elizabethan festival. He was obviously worried about it.

She remembered the conversation she had overheard between Romero and Schotter. Romero had wanted Schotter to work with him on the medieval fair, but Schotter had firmly turned him down. After hearing Romero's flashy plans, Nancy wasn't surprised that Schotter had not been interested.

She wondered if Romero's strong determination could drive him to vandalizing the festival. It was only through luck that no one had been seriously hurt. Had anyone been hurt, the troupe might decide never to return to River Heights.

Nancy decided to spend the rest of the afternoon at home. Hannah, who was still a bit shaken from the previous night's attempted break-in, would appreciate the company. And a few quiet hours would be just the thing to take her mind off the festival for a while.

Nancy awoke early Thursday with a fresh sense of determination. With the festival in town for only three more days, she was impatient to unmask the mysterious note writer. After showering, she called Bess's house. George, who had spent her day off helping J.Z. with some odds and ends, answered.

"You should get an award for being Super-Volunteer," Nancy teased.

George groaned wearily. "I figure with all the construction tips I've been getting from J.Z., I should be able to build my own house someday," she said. "Or at least my own balcony."

Nancy laughed. "Maybe then you could find *your* Romeo," she said. She told George about her meeting with Louis Romero, and then asked if anything unusual had happened on the festival grounds during the break.

"Well, Dean Batlan drove everyone crazy," George said. "He ordered people around and told them what they were doing wrong. And, of course, he managed to complain about being underpaid every chance he got," she finished.

"Hmm," Nancy murmured, taking in this information with interest.

"You know, Josh Forster may be a little pompous himself," George said, "but he's the only one who's able to put Dean in his place. I don't think Dean likes him, but he seems to listen to him."

"Was Martine around yesterday?" Nancy asked.

"I only saw her once," George said. "She was complaining to Schotter about someone going through her trailer."

"What happened?" Nancy said excitedly.

82

"I'm sorry, Nancy, but that's about all I know," George said. "I heard Martine and Schotter arguing, but I couldn't stay around to listen. I had nails to pound and goblets to shine," she said in a tired voice.

"Well, try not to work too hard today," Nancy advised her friend. "I'll pick you and Bess up at eleven-thirty."

With Hannah's help, Nancy put on her high-necked, puffy-sleeved costume again and slipped the ruby ring back on her finger. "It's fun to do this for a week," she said to Hannah, "but I'm sure glad women don't dress like this anymore. I can't imagine wearing this heavy outfit every day!"

On their way to the festival, Nancy told her friends about her conversation with Romero. "I have to find Philip Schotter as soon as we get there," Nancy finished.

Nancy was pleased to find Schotter inside his trailer, just hanging up the phone.

"Come on in, Nancy," he said in a friendly voice. "I keep meaning to check in with you, but I can't seem to find a spare minute." He glanced at his watch. "In fact, I've barely got one now."

"I have just a few questions," Nancy said.

"Of course, of course," Schotter said. "I'll tell you—this note writer is really getting to me." He lowered his voice a bit. "I'm afraid he or she

83

wants to hurt someone, and I don't know what I'd do if that happened." He rubbed his creased forehead. "I'd feel that it was all my fault."

Nancy nodded sympathetically and then said, "I heard Martine DeVries mention something about her contract with the festival. Is there something unusual about it?"

Schotter sighed. "I know Martine is still angry about that," he said wearily. "Martine originally wanted a two-year contract with the festival. That would mean her contract would run through two seasons, each of which goes from April to October. She wanted to feel that people would begin to associate the Elizabethan festival with her—Queen Elizabeth."

"And I assume she didn't get that two-year contract?" Nancy asked.

Schotter shook his head. "The role of Queen Elizabeth was originally intended to be a role of honor. We wanted to give it to an established actress, one who had a solid reputation and who understood the flavor of the festival."

Nancy looked confused. "Doesn't Martine meet those requirements?"

"Yes," Schotter answered. "But since the role is meant to be honorary, and doesn't have required lines to learn, as a play does, we thought the role could be a rotating one. We were hoping that other distinguished actresses might like the chance to play Queen Elizabeth in the upcoming seasons. We thought it would be a nice honor for them," he explained.

"But Martine didn't agree to that?" Nancy guessed.

"Well, she did at first," Schotter said. "Or at least I thought so. But after she had been queen in a couple of different cities, she acted as if she'd been told the role was all hers. She said she wouldn't have agreed to do it if she had known it was only a temporary role."

"So did you give her a contract?" Nancy asked.

Schotter sat back and sighed. "Not right away. Martine got very angry with me and said she wouldn't settle for anything less than a two-year contract. But I couldn't do that. We finally agreed that she would play the role for the summer, and that we'd come to a decision after that."

"Was she satisfied with that?" Nancy asked.

"I'm afraid not," Schotter said. "She said I was only trying to make her look bad—as if she had to beg for a position she deserved. She says she won't let me forget it." He paused for a moment, looking thoughtful. "Martine is a very talented actress. I respect her," he said, "though I don't think she believes I do."

The director was lost in thought for a moment. Then he suddenly looked at his watch. "Late again!" he exclaimed. "Sorry, Nancy, but I have to run."

"Just two more questions," Nancy said as

85

Schotter stood up. "Do you plan to give Martine an extended contract?" she asked.

"I don't know," he said. "The producers and I are still talking about it."

Nancy nodded. "One more thing. Does anyone else have a key to your office?" she said as she stood up.

Schotter shrugged. "Well, J.Z. and Josh often have to run in here, but they borrow *my* key. They're never in here for more than a few minutes at a time. I usually leave it unlocked during the day so I can run in and out and so the troupe members can use the phone."

Nancy left the director's office in deep thought. Schotter had confirmed her suspicions. Martine resented the director's refusal to make her a permanent part of the festival. And Martine was well known for her fits of anger. Perhaps if she can't stay with the festival, Nancy thought, she'll make sure the festival can't stay around.

As she continued walking, Nancy remembered George's comment about Martine having complained about someone going through her trailer. Maybe that was just another way to throw suspicion from herself. Come to think of it—maybe that held true for the falling litter, too. But Nancy reminded herself that Martine might also be telling the truth.

"Oh!" Nancy looked up to see that she had almost walked right into Bess.

"I've been looking all over for you," Bess said. "We're supposed to be with the queen at the hunting-party picnic, remember? They're heading off toward the woods."

Nancy had nearly forgotten about the afternoon's hunting party. The "hunt" was really more like a picnic in the woods. The spectators would be able to watch troupe members demonstrate sixteenth-century hunting techniques. Of course, they wouldn't be shooting at real birds and animals. People were encouraged to buy food at the snack stand and bring it along.

Nancy and Bess hurried to join the procession that was already heading toward the woods. The group walked across a grassy area in between the town square and the trailers, then made its way to a clearing.

Blankets were spread on the ground for those who wanted to eat. The queen, of course, had a small chair to sit on while members of her court sat on mats around her. Martine fanned herself with her beloved fan and fan holder, watching the others with a fixed smile on her face.

The "noblemen" began to blow hunting horns, signaling people to gather around them. When they had several spectators, the men began to explain how actual hunts were conducted. Another group had gathered around a troupe member who had a trained hawk perched on his arm. They were listening to him describe the sixteenth-century sport of hawking. Josh Forster wandered about, answering historical questions.

Nancy and Bess decided to join a few other ladies-in-waiting who were sitting on a blanket, munching on biscuits and cold chicken. As Nancy and Bess approached the group, Nancy commented on Dean Batlan, who was posing for photographs and signing autographs.

Bess rolled her eyes as she watched Dean. "I think he's giving autographs to people who don't even know who he is," she remarked.

Nancy laughed. "He seems to be trying hard to make sure *everyone* knows who he is," she said. She paused and glanced back at Dean as he made his way through the crowd and finally disappeared from view. Her gaze shifted to the woods beyond the clearing, and she admired the shafts of soft sunlight falling on the trees. Then Nancy approached the ladies-in-waiting seated under a large oak tree and said, "Mind if we join you?"

Suddenly Nancy heard a sharp whizzing noise near her ear. She flinched in surprise and felt a rush of air on her cheek.

Looking to her left, she let out a gasp. Lodged in the tree trunk, only inches from her head, was a quivering arrow!

10

A Pointed Warning

Hearing Nancy's gasp, Bess and the other ladies-in-waiting followed her gaze toward the arrow firmly planted in the tree. Several cries were heard, and the women jumped up from the blanket, scattering behind trees.

Nancy studied the angle of the arrow. It indicated that it must have been shot from a clump of trees in the distance. Or had one of the hunting demonstrators shot it accidentally? But who? Nancy spent a breathless few seconds looking for any movement from the trees.

"Nancy, get out of the way!" Bess urged from behind a tree. "Another one could be coming."

Nancy hesitated. The troupe member in charge of the hunting demonstration, after hearing the shrieks, had asked the group to stay together while he checked out the commotion.

Nancy didn't want to lose any more time. With

a solid tug, she pulled the short arrow from the tree trunk. Its small, sharp point glinted in the sunlight.

Nancy took off toward the clump of trees with Bess and the others looking after her. The full Elizabethan skirt made it difficult to run. She lifted the long dress and made her way through the trees, on the lookout for any sign of another person.

After a few moments Nancy slowed down to a walk, casting cautious glances around her. There was still no one in sight. She saw the white outline of a trailer through the trees ahead of her. She realized that she must be approaching the back side of the rows of trailers. She stopped, realizing that this had to be the direction from which the arrow had come. She wondered if it was just a coincidence that the cast and crew trailers were so close to the area from which the arrow came.

On the other hand, she couldn't be sure that she followed the exact line of the arrow. She turned around and headed back toward the picnic area, taking a slightly different path. She worked her way down a line of trees, until a large object near one of the trees caught her eye.

She stooped down for a closer look. It was a weapon. Nancy recognized it as a crossbow—a sixteenth-century weapon that was like a combination of a rifle and a bow and arrow. It shot arrows like the one she held in her hand. Apparently, someone had dropped the crossbow after the single arrow had been shot.

Carefully Nancy picked up the crossbow and did a quick search of the area around it, half expecting to find another note. Having discovered nothing but grass and twigs, she made her way back to the picnic area.

The hunting and picnic area soon came into view. Nancy paused for a moment, staring at the tree that the arrow had hit. From where she was standing, there was an unobstructed line to the tree. An arrow could easily have been shot from that point.

But she realized that someone had to have taken careful aim to avoid hitting the many trees that surrounded the clearing. The shot could hardly have been an accident. Someone had been deliberately aiming the crossbow at the place where she had been sitting.

Was I the target? Nancy thought. She found it hard to believe that the arrow could have been aimed at any of the other ladies-in-waiting.

Looking around, Nancy caught sight of Martine, who had been sitting near Nancy and the others when the arrow hit. She couldn't have shot the crossbow—unless, Nancy thought, she had someone working for her.

Nancy remembered watching Dean Batlan work his way through the crowd at the hunting party. In fact, she recalled, he had insisted on coming to the picnic. But he had disappeared from view just before the arrow had hit the tree. Nancy wondered if he could have been heading for the woods.

"Oh, Nancy, there you are." Nancy turned to see Bess coming toward her. "I was beginning to worry," Bess said. She looked down at the crossbow Nancy was carrying. "What's *that?*"

"It's a crossbow," Nancy said. "I found it in the woods. I think whoever shot at us dropped it as he or she was running away."

"Shot at us!" Bess exclaimed. "Do you think someone was trying to hit one of us?" she said fearfully.

"I'm not sure," Nancy admitted. "What's happening here?"

"The party's breaking up," Bess said. "The play is starting soon, so they're leading people back to the main grounds. I think there's still time to catch the other festival activities going on now. There's dancing, sonnet readings, and other stuff at the town square."

"Do all the spectators know about the arrow?" Nancy asked.

Bess shook her head. "I don't think so. People were spread out, so only the ones near us seemed to know what was going on. But they weren't very happy about it. Some families with small children left right away." Bess stopped and added in a worried voice, "And I don't blame them. Nancy, this festival is getting awfully dangerous!"

Nancy had to agree. "Bess, I want to ask J.Z. about this crossbow. Do you want to come along?"

"No. What I want to do is to find a safe place around here," Bess said. "My heart is still racing. I'm going to go backstage and rest on one of the cots before the play."

Nancy said goodbye to Bess and headed for Schotter's trailer. J.Z. and Josh Forster were the only ones there. They were discussing the shot at the hunting party. Nancy handed the crossbow and arrow to J.Z., who took the weapon from her in surprise.

"How in the world did someone get hold of this?" J.Z. asked. "It was supposed to be locked in the closet."

"Could it have been accidentally mixed in with the other weapons taken to the hunting party?" Nancy asked.

J.Z. shook his head. "The only real weapons that were supposed to be there were the pistols, so we could demonstrate the gunpowder loading," he said. "We didn't want to risk having a spectator accidentally pick up a real weapon. The hunting party is usually crowded and confusing, and it's hard to have a supervised demonstration," he explained.

93

"So all the weapons the actors were using this afternoon were replicas?" Nancy said.

J.Z. nodded. "The crew designs them to look very real, but the fake swords, for example, have very dull edges. And the fake crossbows don't have a spring so the arrows can't be fired."

"It seems, Miss Drew," Josh interrupted, "that you are chasing a very clever festival foe. He or she seems to be everywhere at once, and yet nowhere to be found." His voice, as usual, was even and controlled.

As Nancy considered Josh's words, George suddenly appeared at the door of the trailer. "Hi, Nancy," she said in surprise. "I heard about the arrow. I'm glad no one got hurt." George turned to J.Z. "You're needed backstage. The show's going to start soon."

"Okay. Thanks, George," J.Z. said. He put the crossbow and arrow in the closet, then headed for the door. "I'm glad you found that crossbow," he said to Nancy. "I wouldn't want some kid finding it in the woods later."

"Yes," Josh Forster agreed, "we're certainly fortunate to have your services." Then they all stepped out of the trailer, and J.Z. locked the door behind them.

Nancy and George followed the two men to the theater, staying a bit behind them. In a low voice Nancy repeated what J.Z. had told her about the weapons.

94

George nodded. "He's right. The crew only took fakes to that hunting party. No one backstage can understand where the arrow came from."

"Where was J.Z. during the hunting party?" Nancy asked.

"I saw him backstage with Schotter," George said.

Nancy and George separated when they reached the backstage tent, where actors were warming up for the play. Nancy found Bess resting on a cot. "I think the procession is starting soon," she said. "C'mon, Bess. We should go line up."

Reluctantly Bess stood up. "Maybe we should skip the play tonight," she said hesitantly. She looked worried.

"Why?" Nancy said in surprise. "I thought you liked watching the play."

"I do," Bess said. "But, well . . . what if this hunter comes back? I don't want to be a sitting duck in the front row," she added.

"I understand," Nancy said, putting her arm around her friend. "I'm worried, too. But I want to put a stop to this. I can't help feeling there's something I'm overlooking. I think I need to be here for the play."

Bess sighed. "Oh, all right," she said. "Let's just try not to be too conspicuous, okay?"

"Okay," Nancy said.

A short while later Nancy and Bess were once again caught up in the drama of *Romeo and Juliet*. That evening's performance went well, and the festival completed its fourth day without any other mishaps.

Nancy reached home feeling very tired. She pulled into her driveway and, keys in hand, climbed the steps to her front door. Standing on the top step, she stopped and drew in her breath.

Stuck to the front door was a dagger, holding a note. The note was written in large black type. With her heart hammering in her chest, Nancy read the note.

"Is this a dagger which I see before me . . . ?"
It is indeed, and one meant especially
    for you.
You were lucky this afternoon, Nancy Drew.
I may have missed once, but I usually get
    my prey,
So here's a friendly warning:
Stay out of my way!

11

Much Ado About Something

Nancy shuddered as she reread the note. Then she pulled the long ivory-colored sleeve of her dress over her hand and carefully removed the dagger from the door, trying not to smudge any fingerprints. She caught the note and took both items inside the house.

Sitting down in the living room, Nancy thought about the note. She knew now that she had definitely been the target of the arrow at the hunting party. She breathed a sigh of relief, thankful that the writer's aim had not been very precise. But then, on a darker note, she realized that the writer knew who she was and where she lived. This incident meant that the person who was at her bedroom window must be connected to the trouble at the festival. Most likely, the note writer and the intruder were the same person— or were, at least, working with the same person.

So far there had been five notes written, she thought. Each one gave a warning in rhyme. And each note had accompanied an incident meant to hurt someone and create a disturbance at the festival.

There were at least three people she knew who might want to damage the festival—Martine DeVries, Dean Batlan, and Louis Romero. All of them had indicated that they were angry at the festival or its director in some way.

But while any of them might try to hurt the festival while it was in River Heights, Nancy couldn't understand why one of them would want to hurt *her*. She didn't think any of them knew she was a detective. Besides, she thought, as she absentmindedly slid the ruby ring on and off her finger, Dean or Martine would have had a hard time beating her home after the play. Nancy and Bess had left the festival grounds just after the play ended. And the note had to have been placed sometime between the shooting of the arrow and her arrival home.

Louis Romero might have had time, Nancy speculated. She hadn't seen him at that evening's performance of *Romeo and Juliet*. But that would mean he was also the one who had tried to break into her house Tuesday night. When Nancy had visited Romero's office on Wednesday, he hadn't given any sign that he was guilty. Maybe Romero's just a good actor, she thought. Her other suspects were good actors, too, which made the case even more difficult.

She got up from the chair and headed upstairs to get ready for bed. She still felt that there was something she was missing—something she just wasn't seeing. And now that she knew she had become a target of the note writer, she had to find that something more than ever. She resolved to find it at the festival the next day.

By noon on Friday the sky was a clear blue, without a cloud. Her Majesty's Players had been lucky to have such nice weather all week, Nancy thought as she drove to Bess's house.

A few minutes later Bess and George were climbing into the Mustang with cheerful greetings. Before Nancy pulled away from the curb, she held up the dagger that had been stuck to her front door. She had placed it in a clear plastic bag.

"Do you recognize this?" she asked George.

While George tried to get a better look at the dagger, Bess let out a squeal of surprise. "A knife? Oh, Nancy, I'm almost afraid to ask where you got that."

"Well, actually it's a dagger," Nancy said. "It was stuck to my front door along with this note when I got home last night."

George and Bess read over the note with the old-fashioned lettering. Bess looked up with

99

wide eyes. "Well, that does it," she said quietly and firmly. "Let's just go turn in our costumes and say goodbye to the festival."

"I don't always agree with Bess," George said, "but I think she might be right, Nancy. Are you sure it's safe to go back to the festival? Things are getting pretty serious."

"I think our note writer is going to continue whether I'm there or not," Nancy said. "And as long as that person keeps causing trouble, everybody at the festival is in danger. What I'd like to do is stop by the police station and drop off this dagger. Maybe the police can check for fingerprints. George, have you ever seen anyone with a dagger like this at the festival?"

George shook her head. "In the first place, the blade on that dagger is real. All the ones I've seen at the festival have been fakes. And the handle on this one seems more elaborate than the others."

"I thought so, too," Nancy said, nodding. "I wonder how our note writer got his or her hands on it."

Bess shuddered. "I don't even want to think about that," she said. "Let's just hope the person doesn't have more where this came from."

"George, maybe you could check with J.Z. to see if there's anything missing from Schotter's closet," Nancy suggested.

George nodded. "No problem."

Bess and George waited in the car while Nancy

100

ran into the police station. She mentioned to Chief McGinnis that Officers DelRio and Wilkerson had checked out the attempted break-in earlier in the week, and that the dagger might be connected to that incident. A few minutes later she was back in the car, driving her friends to the festival.

Bess and George stopped to watch a clown act while Nancy went in search of Dean Batlan's trailer. Ever since the first day, when she had heard him boasting, she had been meaning to find out more about him.

In the first row of trailers she found a small trailer with Dean's name on a sign hanging on the door. She knocked. There was no answer. A few seconds later she knocked again. "Mr. Batlan?" she called out.

Nancy waited a bit longer, and then, looking around her, tried turning the doorknob. To her surprise, the door opened readily. She wondered if Dean, like Schotter, often left his door open.

Poking her head into the trailer, she called out, "Dean?" No one answered. Nancy stepped inside, closed the door behind her, and looked around the small interior.

To the right, at the back end of the trailer, was a paneled closet. Across from the closet was a kitchenette, with a small refrigerator and stove, and next to the kitchenette was a small bathroom.

A cot was pushed against one wall, and strewn

about it were several articles of clothing and costume accessories.

Along the other wall was a dressing table with a large mirror over it. Nancy began looking through the items scattered on the dressing table. There were bottles of stage makeup, publicity photos, and several typed pages of Dean's *Romeo and Juliet* script. Certain lines had been underlined and notes had been written in the margins. Nancy noticed that the publicity photos were of Dean himself, already autographed. Suddenly a large black binder in the corner of the table caught her eye.

Bending over the binder, Nancy opened it and quickly began to leaf through its many papers. The binder evidently stored Dean's official documents and personal mementos. Nancy skimmed through old newspaper clippings of theater reviews, old contracts, and business letters. She noticed that most of the materials were five to ten years old. Batlan's acting had been well received years ago, but it looked as if he had not done much significant work since then.

Just as Nancy was about to close the binder, she noticed a name scrawled at the bottom of one page. Excitedly she stared at a letter signed by Louis Romero.

Nancy took in a short breath and was about to read the letter when she heard heavy footsteps.

She glanced out the window and jumped back. Dean Batlan had returned.

Slamming the binder shut, Nancy looked around the small trailer in desperation. Deciding there was nowhere to hide, she prepared to face Dean Batlan, hoping he'd believe a story about being in the wrong trailer.

But in the next instant Nancy heard a scream coming from outside. She ran to the small window and saw Dean Batlan running off in the direction of the scream.

Nancy didn't waste any time. She hurried out of Dean's trailer and followed him toward the scream. She noticed other cast and crew members heading in that direction, too.

As Nancy neared the middle section of the first row of trailers, she almost collided with Martine DeVries, who had suddenly appeared from behind a trailer.

Martine's eyes were wide with fright as she stood clutching her throat. "Someone's trying to kill me!" she gasped.

12

The Play's the Thing

Nancy, Dean, and the other cast and crew members gathered around a distraught Martine. The actress was coughing and breathing erratically. "I don't know where he came from," she said, her voice sounding even deeper than usual.

"He?" Nancy asked.

"I think it was a he," Martine said. "I never got a look at the person's face," she said, her breath coming in gasps. "He was very strong," she added.

"Just slow down and tell us what happened," Joanna Messerman said.

"I stepped out of my trailer, and the next thing I knew, someone was grabbing my neck from behind," Martine said, still rubbing her neck. "The person wrapped his hands around my neck tighter and tighter, trying to strangle me. His hands were pushing against this brooch I was wearing, and it was cutting into my neck."

104

Martine's hand flew up to her neck to feel for the brooch, a round pin with small sapphire stones set in it. "Thank goodness it's still here," she said, touching the beautiful, blue-stoned pin.

"And then what happened?" Dean said impatiently.

"Well, I couldn't breathe, obviously!" Martine retorted angrily. "He was choking me so hard I thought I was going to pass out. I threw back my elbow and hit him in the ribs. He let go, and I tried to scream." She paused for a moment, still breathing heavily. "No sound would come out, though. I kept trying to get my voice to work, but I could hardly breathe. I started running, and after a few more tries, a scream finally came out." Martine stopped, looking tired and scared.

"What happened to your attacker?" Nancy asked gently.

Martine shrugged. "I think he ran off. After I elbowed him, I caught a quick glance. I think he was wearing black, and it looked as if he had one of the black masks from the props trailer covering his face."

"Do you feel pretty certain it was a man?" Nancy asked.

"Well, whoever it was seemed bigger and stronger than I. I think it was a man, but I didn't get a good look," Martine replied.

While the others escorted Martine back to her trailer, Nancy headed toward the back row of trailers, in the direction Martine had thought her attacker had gone. But after a few minutes of searching the spaces between the trailers for something or someone unusual, she gave up. The attacker had had too great a head start.

Nancy walked back to Martine's trailer, thinking about the actress's story. Nancy had no reason to doubt her. Martine was obviously very upset, and her troubled breathing and the rough, red marks on her neck seemed to be solid proof of an attack.

When Nancy reached the trailer, she found Martine sitting up on her bed. Though she seemed to be a bit less shaken, it was clear that the attack had very much affected her. As she spoke to Schotter, who had recently arrived, there were tears in her eyes.

"I don't know what's going on around here," Martine said quietly, "but you'd better do something about it, Philip. Until this is resolved, I'm not participating in one more event."

"Martine, I know you're scared," Schotter said sympathetically. "And to be honest, this makes me nervous, too. I'm very sorry about what happened. But we can't simply go into hiding or pack up and leave—"

Martine interrupted the director. "But I'm not going to give somebody another opportunity to get to me. By going to the play or even just walking around the town square, I'm asking for trouble."

"Actually, you might be safer at the play," Nancy put in. "You'll be surrounded by other actors and volunteers. Someone would have a hard time getting to you in those circumstances. After all," Nancy pointed out, "it was when you were alone in your trailer that you were attacked."

Martine was about to argue with Nancy when Schotter cut in.

"Nancy's right, you know," Schotter said quickly. "There's safety in numbers. We can make sure that you're never alone."

Martine considered the director's words for a few seconds. Then she said, "All right. I'll go to the play, but I'm not entering the theater by procession. I just want to come in with the rest of the audience. And I want to leave as soon as the play ends, with everyone else. Got that?" she said, pointing a finger at Schotter.

"Okay, you got it," Schotter said, putting his hands up. "No procession, no announcements— just another audience member. I'll go to my trailer and report your assault to the police. And don't worry—I'm sure everything will be fine," he said, his voice sounding less confident than his words.

Nancy had been only half listening to Schotter

107

and Martine. Her mind had drifted back to Dean Batlan's trailer. She had been on the verge of finding out what Louis Romero had written to Dean Batlan when Martine had screamed. Now Nancy desperately wanted to get back to that letter.

Quietly Nancy slipped out of Martine's trailer and hurried down the row to Dean's. Looking around cautiously, she opened the door of the trailer and went in. She left the door open a crack so she could keep an eye out for Dean or anyone else.

Working fast, Nancy grabbed the black binder and flipped to the letter that bore Louis Romero's signature. Skimming through the letter, she noticed that it had Monday's date at the top. Her eyes opened wider and wider as she read the few short paragraphs. Louis Romero was writing to offer Dean Batlan a position in the medieval fair.

Nancy read over the paragraphs again, to make sure she wasn't mistaken. She wasn't. Romero was definitely asking Dean to sign on with him. At the bottom of the page Nancy's eyes rested on a handwritten line written in pencil: "Talk to Phil." Nancy stared at the line, her heart beating so hard she was sure it could be heard outside.

Then she heard several different voices coming closer and closer to Dean's trailer. Nancy slammed the black binder shut and put it back on the dressing table where she'd found it. Then she left the trailer.

Thinking no one had seen her, she began to walk in the opposite direction of the voices. She was startled by Dean Batlan's loud voice behind her. "Hey! You there—what are you doing?"

Trying to look innocent, Nancy turned around slowly. "Are you talking to me?" she asked in a surprised voice.

"Of course I am," Dean thundered. "What were you doing in my trailer?"

"*Your* trailer?" Nancy asked, her voice full of astonishment. "Oh, I'm so sorry, Mr. Batlan, I had no idea that that was your trailer. I got so confused—I'm supposed to be in the costume trailer. These trailers all look so much alike, and I'm late already, and oh! I'm just so sorry, if I had known it was yours, I never would have gone near it," Nancy said in a confused flurry. She gave Dean a quick smile and skipped off before he could say another word.

When Nancy had gotten past the trailer rows, she slowed down and let out a huge breath. She hoped Dean had bought her innocent act. At any rate, she thought, Dean had more important things to think about—like Romero's offer.

She figured that Dean must have written in the line "Talk to Phil." Phil had to be Philip Schotter. But was Dean seriously considering whether or not to accept the offer? Perhaps Dean wanted to make sure Schotter knew that he was being offered big money and a permanent part in Romero's production. Even if Dean *was* going to turn down the offer, he might want Schotter to think he was interested. If Dean wanted more money from the Elizabethan festival, Nancy reasoned, this might be a good way to convince Schotter that he was worth it. Romero's offer could be used as a bargaining tool to prove that Dean was still a valued actor.

But even as she became more suspicious of Dean, she reflected that he couldn't have been Martine's attacker. She had heard his voice outside the trailer just before Martine had screamed. And he had stayed with Martine after she had told her story, showing real concern.

Nancy headed into the backstage tent to find Bess and George. She found the cousins sitting in a corner of the tent, enjoying sandwiches and lemonade.

"I know that look on your face," George said to Nancy. "You've figured something out. What's up?"

Nancy laughed. "Are you sure you can't read my mind?" She sat down with them and told them about Martine's attack and her visit to Dean's trailer.

"These attacks are getting worse," Bess said fearfully. "First you have an arrow shot at you and a dagger stuck on your door, and now Martine gets strangled."

"That's assuming the same person was responsible for both attacks," George said. "As Nancy said, nobody found a note near Martine's attack. Maybe that was a separate incident. I know a few people around here who have probably felt like strangling Martine from time to time."

"But do you think any of those people would actually do something like that?" Nancy asked.

George shook her head. "No, I don't. Martine can be exasperating, but I think most people do seem to respect her."

"So it *could* be the same person," Bess said slowly. "But it isn't Dean, right?" she asked Nancy.

Nancy sighed in frustration. "There may be other things about him I don't know yet." She paused. "It seems pretty unlikely that he's involved, though," she admitted.

A troupe member was making his way through the tent, informing everyone that the play was about to start. Bess and George finished eating, and Bess and Nancy made their way to their front-row seats.

Martine sat on Nancy's left. The actress seemed extremely nervous. Nancy didn't blame her. But she relaxed a little when the play began. She became absorbed in the crowded scene in which attendants and members of the Montague

111

and Capulet families were feuding with each other. Nancy, however, found it difficult to concentrate on the play at all. She couldn't stop thinking about the afternoon's events.

She knew that someone had deliberately shot an arrow at her, and that someone had physically attacked Martine, as well.

Nancy thought back to the other incidents. The damaged weapons rack, which had fallen on three troupe members, would have fallen no matter who had used it. But the broken litter had to be directed at Martine. The note that accompanied it mentioned the queen specifically.

The sabotaged balcony could only have affected Joanna Messerman, who was playing Juliet. But the note that Nancy had found on the balcony hadn't mentioned Joanna or Juliet. It had been a warning about bringing the whole show down. And the note left at the scene of the switched rapiers hadn't mentioned anyone, either.

So the only sure targets seemed to be Nancy and Martine. But if someone—Romero, maybe—was simply trying to damage the festival, there was no need for personal attacks. The festival was leaving River Heights after tomorrow, anyway. Why would someone be after her and Martine?

Nancy glanced at Martine out of the corner of her eye. The actress was calmly fanning herself, her eyes fixed on the stage. Nancy smiled.

Martine hadn't parted with her bejeweled fan holder ever since she and Bess had found it in the locked storage trailer. The line of rubies trailing from the holder sparkled as the fan moved back and forth.

Suddenly Nancy sat bolt upright in her seat. She grabbed Bess's arm and squeezed it.

"What is it?" Bess whispered.

"I think I know why someone is after Martine!" Nancy said excitedly.

13

The Real Thing?

"Nancy, what are you talking about?" Bess whispered.

Nancy tried to keep her excitement down so she wouldn't attract any attention. Placing her right hand on Bess's arm, she looked down at the ruby ring on her third finger, then looked back up at Bess.

"The jewels, Bess. What if they're real?" Nancy whispered.

"Real?" Bess whispered back. "But these are costume pieces," she said, looking at Nancy in confusion.

"That's what everyone *thinks*," Nancy said. "I'll tell you what I think after the play." She looked at the emerald earrings Bess was wearing. Then she turned to look at Martine's brooch and fan holder. Perhaps these pieces aren't just well-made imitations, after all, Nancy thought. Maybe that's the reason she had found them hidden away together in the metal box in the trunk.

Nancy's head was spinning as she considered this possibility. If the jewels *were* real, it would certainly explain why Martine's fan holder, which the actress had claimed was stolen when her litter broke, turned up inside the trunk. And it would explain why Martine had felt her attacker grabbing for her brooch when she was being strangled. Someone had been trying to get to the jewelry—not to Martine.

Nancy absently clapped a couple of times as the third act came to an end. She was warning herself not to jump to conclusions. Her idea might explain why someone had tried to break into her house. The intruder could have been coming after the ring. But it didn't explain the broken balcony or the falling weapons rack. Those things had happened before she and Bess had found the jewels. Even if she and Bess *had* actually discovered a would-be thief's hiding place, then Nancy was still left with the question of what the earlier notes and incidents meant.

And there was a more frightening question, too. Nancy had been shot at with an arrow. And Martine had been choked. Was someone so desperate for the jewelry that he or she was willing to physically harm the people wearing it?

Bess had been giving Nancy confused looks

115

during the play, and when it was finally over, she grabbed Nancy's arm. "What's going on?" Bess asked, over the applause.

"I'll tell you in a minute," Nancy said. People were beginning to leave the theater.

As Martine rose to leave, Nancy approached her. "Excuse me, Martine," she said politely. "I've been admiring your fan and fan holder, and I wondered if I could borrow them overnight. Of course, I'd return them to you before tomorrow afternoon's activities, but I—"

"No," Martine said abruptly. "I'm not interested in some teenage accessory swapping," she said, turning away.

Nancy felt frustrated. She didn't want to tell Martine of her suspicions until she'd had a chance to get some real evidence. But she also wanted to bring the fan holder and the other jewels to a jewelry appraiser the next morning.

Martine was intent on leaving the theater, though. Before Nancy could say another word, the actress had already made her way backstage.

Sighing, Nancy turned to find Bess staring at her with her hands on her hips. "Will you please tell me what is going on with these jewels?" Bess asked with a note of exasperation.

"Yes," Nancy said, "but not here. Let's get George and talk in the car."

The two girls found George backstage, and a few minutes later the three of them were heading toward the parking lot. They climbed in the car, and the two cousins listened in surprise as Nancy told them she thought the jewelry might be authentic.

Bess took off her earrings and inspected them. "They do look very well made," she admitted.

"But these are just suspicions," Nancy warned. "I need some facts to back me up—and I need them quickly. Tomorrow is the last day of the festival." She asked Bess to let her take the emerald earrings home with her. Then the girls planned to go to an appraiser the next morning on their way to the festival.

When Nancy arrived home, she put the emerald earrings and the ruby ring into her father's safe. She didn't want to risk losing the jewels to another intruder. If she was right about the jewels, someone would be desperately trying to get them back now—especially knowing that the jewels would only be in River Heights for one more day.

Nancy found a telephone message for her on the kitchen counter. It said that the police department had called with some discouraging news. Because of the ornate design of the old-fashioned dagger, no fingerprints had been retrieved from the weapon.

Nancy awoke the next morning trying to remember when she had fallen asleep. The last thing she remembered was lying on her bed, thinking about the festival. She realized that exhaustion must have overtaken her.

After showering, she called Bess, who told her that George had gone early to the festival. The two girls decided to wear jeans to the appraiser's office. They could change into their costumes at the festival.

About a half hour later Nancy and Bess were sitting across a desk from the jewelry appraiser, Ms. Bailey. The young woman, dressed in a tidy gray suit, was examining the earrings and ring under a strong desk lamp. With her jeweler's eyepiece, she examined the jewelry carefully. Nancy and Bess sat on the edge of their seats, nervously awaiting her opinion.

After a few moments Ms. Bailey removed her eyepiece and looked up at them. "These are beautiful pieces," she said, "and quite valuable, too. The stones are exquisite."

"You mean they're *real?*" Bess blurted out.

Ms. Bailey looked a bit startled. "Oh, yes. There's no question that the jewels are genuine. And the stones have almost no flaws."

While Bess tried to contain her surprise, Nancy asked, "Could you tell us how old the pieces are? We were wondering if they might be from the Elizabethan period."

Ms. Bailey paused, still looking over the jewelry. "That's a real possibility. I noticed right away that the settings of both items are quite unusual. From this first glance I'd say we're looking at pieces that are hundreds of years old."

Bess let out a little squeal and grabbed Nancy's arm.

"But I can't state that positively right now," Ms. Bailey added quickly. "Before I'd make any kind of verification, I'd have to call in a specialist for a detailed, researched appraisal."

"Would you mind doing that?" Nancy asked.

"Not at all," Ms. Bailey said. "I could make a few phone calls and get someone started on it right away." The appraiser hesitated for a moment. "Are these pieces family heirlooms?" she asked politely.

"Oh, no," Nancy said. "They were donated to the Elizabethan festival that's in town this week. Volunteers were allowed to wear them with their period costumes," she explained.

Ms. Bailey looked surprised. Then she said, "I'll keep the pieces in the safe here until the appraisal is finished. I'll give you a receipt in the meantime."

"Thank you," Nancy said. Then, a bit anxiously, she added, "It's important that we get this information as soon as possible." She wrote her name and phone number on a piece of paper and slid it across the desk to Ms. Bailey. "I'd appreciate it if you could let me know as soon as you find out anything."

Ms. Bailey smiled. "Of course," she said reassuringly. She shook hands with Bess and Nancy, and the two girls left the appraiser's office.

"Nancy, you were right!" Bess exclaimed when they got back into the car. "Someone has been after those jewels the whole time."

"Well, we can't be sure about that," Nancy said, frowning. "We don't know if anyone else knows the jewels are real."

"But somebody must know," Bess said. "Why else would the jewelry have been hidden away in that trailer?"

Nancy didn't answer. "Do you mind if we make another stop?" she said, starting up the car. She pulled a piece of paper from her purse. "I got the name of the woman who donated the jewelry to the festival. Donna Vasquez gave it to me," she said, referring to the costume manager. "A Mrs. Pellworth was the donator. I'd like to talk to her."

"Mrs. Pellworth?" Bess said, as if the name sounded familiar. "Oh, I've heard of her. I think she's always donating stuff to arts projects in town. She sounds like a very generous woman."

Nancy pulled over to a pay phone and got Mrs. Pellworth's address. Minutes later they were driving into a quaint, older section of River Heights. When they reached a two-story red brick house, Nancy parked, and the two girls made their way up a walkway past a neatly kept garden.

Nancy rang the doorbell. The door was opened

120

almost immediately by a kind-looking, elderly woman. "May I help you?" she asked, her eyes bright with expectation. She was hunched over and looked quite old.

Nancy introduced herself and Bess, and explained that they were volunteering for the Elizabethan festival. The woman smiled. "Wonderful!" she exclaimed. "I'll be attending the festival today myself, as a matter of fact." She invited the two girls into a spacious, pastel-colored living room to sit down.

As soon as they were seated in comfortable overstuffed chairs, a trim, blond woman in a white uniform appeared from a hallway. "Is everything all right, Mrs. P?" she asked, eyeing Nancy and Bess a bit suspiciously.

"Oh, yes, Susanna," Mrs. Pellworth said. "These two young ladies are volunteers from the Elizabethan festival."

"I'm Susanna, Mrs. Pellworth's attendant," the woman said in a more relaxed tone. She offered them tea, but they politely declined.

"I apologize for not asking that myself," Mrs. Pellworth said. "I'm afraid I've been very forgetful lately. And I've been having more and more trouble getting around," Mrs. Pellworth explained. "Susanna has been a great help to me." She smiled appreciatively at the attendant.

Susanna came in and sat down next to Mrs. Pellworth. Nancy got right to the point. "As volunteers, Mrs. Pellworth, we've been able to wear some of the jewelry you donated to the festival," she said.

"It's just beautiful," Bess put in. "The pieces add so much to the costumes."

Mrs. Pellworth smiled. "I'm just glad that someone is able to use them," she said. "They've been gathering dust in my attic for so long."

"Are they pieces you purchased yourself, or are they family heirlooms?" Nancy asked.

"Oh, they've been around as long as I can remember," the elderly woman said. "Why, I even remember my great-grandmother wearing them. But you see, I have no children, so I had no one to pass them along to. I decided to give them to the festival so that many people—like yourselves—could enjoy them."

"It was very thoughtful of you," Nancy said, smiling. She paused before asking her next question. "Did you ever have anyone look at them to see if they might be authentic?" she said, trying to sound casual.

Mrs. Pellworth gave a little wave of her hand. "Oh, I never bothered. They've just been sitting around here for so long, I think the only value they have is sentimental. Everyone in my family assumed they were costume pieces," she said.

"Do you know where they came from originally?" Nancy asked.

Mrs. Pellworth shook her head, looking a bit

confused. "I really don't know anything about them. It seems as if they've been around forever."

Mrs. Pellworth leaned back in her chair, suddenly looking very tired. Susanna jumped up, ran to the kitchen, and brought her a glass of water from the kitchen.

Nancy stood up quickly. "Well, Mrs. Pellworth," she said, "we don't want to keep you. We just wanted to thank you again for your generous donation." She signaled to Bess with her eyes.

"Oh, uh, yes," Bess said, jumping to her feet. "Thank you so much, Mrs. Pellworth."

"Well, it always makes me feel good to know people appreciate my silly old things," Mrs. Pellworth said. "I hope to see both of you at the festival this afternoon."

Nancy and Bess got back in the car and headed toward the festival grounds.

"Didn't you want to tell Mrs. Pellworth that the jewels are real?" Bess said.

Nancy shook her head. "I don't think she knows anything about the jewelry, and I didn't want to get her involved until we figure this thing out."

After a few moments of silence Bess spoke up. "So who do you think might be going after these jewels?"

"Well, we pretty much have to count out Martine," Nancy said. "She was really shaken up after someone tried to strangle her. And if she knew that the jewels were real, and wanted to take them, she's had every opportunity to get them back from us," Nancy pointed out. Then, as an afterthought, she said, "Even though she's pretty possessive about her fan holder, she certainly doesn't try to hide it from anyone."

"What about Dean?" Bess asked. "Didn't he say he wanted to bring the festival down?"

"That's just it," Nancy said. "Before yesterday I thought someone was causing this chaos because she or he had some kind of grudge against the festival. That's what the notes implied. So Dean seemed to be a likely suspect."

Nancy paused for a moment. "But if it's true that someone has actually been trying to steal these jewels, then I have to rethink this. Maybe the notes were simply meant to be distractions. And I don't know if Dean would recognize or even be interested in Elizabethan jewelry. After all, Josh is always criticizing him for how little he knows about the period."

Suddenly Nancy's eyes popped open. "Oh, that's it!" she exclaimed. "Josh!"

"Josh what?" Bess replied.

"Josh would know about Elizabethan jewelry, wouldn't he? And wouldn't he have almost every opportunity to go after the pieces?" Nancy asked, her voice rising.

She turned into the festival grounds and drove toward the parking lot. "I don't know why I didn't think of this before," Nancy said. "Bess, we can't waste any time. We've got to find Josh and—"

Nancy didn't have time to finish her sentence. Just as she reached the end of the parking row, a silver sedan bolted out from the trailer area on the right. Nancy expected the car to slow down when the driver saw her, but instead, the car pressed forward, heading straight for Nancy's Mustang!

14

A Player Is Unmasked

Staring in horror at the oncoming car, Nancy automatically jerked the steering wheel to the left, slamming on her brakes at the same time. The Mustang lurched to a stop, and Nancy and Bess were thrown forward in their seats. Bess flung her hands out to the dashboard to catch herself. Both girls turned to see the other car zip by on the right, inches from Nancy's car.

"What on earth is going on?" Bess said in a quivering voice.

Nancy shook her head. "Are you all right?" she asked her friend. Bess's face looked pale.

"I—I think so," Bess said. "That guy must be crazy."

"I know," Nancy said quietly. After unbuckling her seat belt, she opened her door and jumped out. She saw that she had narrowly missed hitting the parked car on her left, the last car in the parking row. Suddenly there was a screech of tires, and Nancy spun around. About fifty feet away she saw the silver sedan make a U-turn and then head back toward them at top speed!

Nancy bent down to warn Bess, who was still in the passenger seat. At the same time Bess noticed the car coming straight toward them. "Nancy!" she screamed.

The car screeched to a stop just in front of Nancy's car. In the next instant the driver jumped out from behind the steering wheel. Nancy found herself looking at Josh Forster.

Josh's face was expressionless. From his side he drew up his right hand. His fingers were wrapped around a dagger, its blade gleaming in the sunlight.

A high-pitched squeal broke the silence, as Bess got out of the car and saw the dagger in Josh's hand.

"Quiet!" Josh snapped at her. He looked around nervously and then pointed the dagger at both girls. "Now that I've got your attention, let's go, Little Miss Detective," he said. His precise, even voice was laced with sarcasm.

Josh pointed the dagger in the direction of the trailers, and Nancy and Bess began walking toward them. Josh followed, looking about every few seconds to make sure no one was watching. He directed the girls to the last row of trailers, which bordered the woods. When they reached a small unit at the end, Josh roughly pushed them inside.

Nancy and Bess stepped into the cramped trailer, which evidently belonged to Josh. A small sofa bed and table were covered with books and papers.

After closing and locking the door behind him, Josh faced Nancy and Bess with a smirk on his face. "Aren't we in costume yet, ladies?"

Nancy and Bess stared at the creative consultant. He no longer looked like the mild-mannered scholar they had seen throughout the week. The tweed jacket and carefully combed hair were gone. His brown hair hung over his wire-rimmed glasses. His eyes flashed wildly, and his mouth was fixed in a mean little smirk.

Bess looked frantically from Josh to Nancy, her lower lip trembling. "Nancy, what's going on?" she whispered.

Without taking her eyes off Josh, Nancy whispered, "Josh wants the jewels we've been wearing, Bess," she said carefully and evenly.

"You were right, then," Bess said.

"Yes," Nancy said. "Josh is the person who's been trying to steal them."

"Oh, very good, *very* good," Josh said, smirking again. "Too bad you're just a little too late."

"I just want to know," Nancy said to Josh, ignoring his remark, "how did you know the jewels were real?"

"Ah," Josh said, raising his eyebrows, "ever the

detective, aren't we, Miss Drew? Well, anyone who has studied Elizabethan history—which is more than I can say for anyone around here—would know right away that those weren't costume pieces. The exquisite settings, the quality of the stones, the unusual designs—I knew they were the real items. I've studied hundreds of photographs of similar pieces," he said confidently.

"When was the first time you saw them?" Nancy asked, keeping her voice calm.

"I was asked to accept them from Mrs. Pellworth, of course," Josh said, a little annoyed. "You forget, Miss Drew, I'm the most trusted person around here. Phil asked me to accompany him and Donna Vasquez to Mrs. Pellworth's house." He paused for a moment, eyeing Nancy suspiciously. Then he shrugged. "I might as well tell you—the two of you will be history soon, anyway."

Nancy heard Bess gasp as Josh went on.

"I knew right then that this was the discovery of a lifetime. That fan holder," he said, shaking his head. "You can never find something made that exquisitely anymore—even as a costume piece. It's extremely rare." Josh had a faraway look in his eyes.

"But the pieces weren't given to *you* at Mrs. Pellworth's, right?" Nancy said.

Josh shook his head and adjusted his wire-rimmed glasses. "Of course not. Donna kept all of them with her. She mixed them in with the costume pieces we already had and then passed them out to the members of the troupe, and even to the volunteers." He rolled his eyes. "Besides, I needed to have time to look over the whole donation carefully. Not all of them are real, you know," he said, gesturing with the dagger.

Nancy was listening carefully to Josh's story. "So that's when you decided to create a commotion by loosening that weapons rack," Nancy said. "You knew everyone would run over to that trailer when the rack fell."

"I just needed enough time to get into Martine's trailer and grab the pieces she had been given," Josh said, shrugging. "Once I had them and could begin studying them, I could tell which ones were real. I have to give Martine credit," he said. "She has a good eye for jewelry. She got a few fakes from Donna, but she also happened to have asked for the only real ones— the earrings, the ring, the brooch, and the fan holder. Unfortunately, Martine had the fan with her when I sneaked into her trailer, and I could only get hold of the earrings, the ring, and the brooch. So I hid those pieces away in the trunk and planned a way to get at the fan."

Bess suddenly spoke up. "Does Martine know the jewelry is real?" she asked in a confused voice.

Nancy shot Bess a warning look. Nancy was worried that Martine could be in danger. She was still in possession of two of the pieces—the fan and the brooch—which were found after Josh had put them in the storage trailer.

Josh waved his hand. "Puh-lease," he said. "She just wanted the best-looking pieces. She doesn't know anything about it."

"And to make sure no one else knew anything about it, you started writing those notes, to make it look as if someone were trying to hurt the festival," Nancy put in.

Josh slowly worked his mouth into a wide smile as he pointed the dagger at Nancy. "Now, that," he said, "was a stroke of genius on my part."

Nancy looked at the mousy creative consultant with mounting disgust. She could feel her anger rise, but she told herself to keep calm and find out as much as she could from Josh. "And since you wanted to get the fan holder away from Martine," she went on, "you tampered with the litter so she'd fall."

Josh nodded, still smiling. "After that I had all the real pieces in what I thought was a safe place—until you found them. But the notes were really working. Nobody even paid the slightest attention to the missing jewelry. So I kept it up by unscrewing the balcony." He was obviously pleased with himself. "It was perfect. It fell apart right in the middle of the play!"

"That's sick!" Bess blurted out. "Joanna could have really been hurt."

Josh shrugged. "If anything, Dean was the one

131

to get hurt. She landed right on top of him. And that wouldn't have been a great loss," he added.

"And the rapier switch must have been easy," Nancy said. "You have access to Schotter's office."

"The whole thing had been so easy up to that point," Josh said. "That's why I was so surprised to see the two of you wearing the jewels. I knew you must have found the trunk." He pulled in his breath. "But that doesn't matter now," he added, pointing the dagger at Nancy and Bess. "Now I can get them back."

"But we don't have them!" Bess wailed.

"No," Josh said coolly, "but right after the performance, you'll lead me to them. In fact, we may even be able to get to them before the performance ends, if Martine cooperates."

"What does Martine have to do with it?" Nancy said.

Josh smirked at Nancy. "You don't expect me to leave without my fan holder and brooch, do you? Martine is going to have to learn to be a little less stubborn. But I think," he said, smiling and waving the dagger, "I can convince her of that this evening."

Nancy looked at Josh sharply. "Did you say 'leave'? Are you planning on leaving the festival?"

Josh let out a soft little chuckle. "Tut, tut, Miss Drew. I'd have expected you to figure that out by now. It doesn't do me any good to sit around here with the jewelry, does it? Someone might get suspicious. Besides, it wouldn't be very profitable. I plan to meet my jewelry buyer tonight."

Josh quickly glanced down at his watch. "Ah! No time to waste," he said, looking up. "Hang on, ladies—you're going for a ride," he said with a nasty smile. Then he backed out of the trailer and closed the door.

"What does he mean?" Bess asked fearfully. The girls heard Josh lock the door from the outside.

"I don't know," Nancy said grimly. "But I have a feeling we're about to find out."

Suddenly the girls heard a car starting up outside. The sound of the engine grew louder as the car slowly pulled close to the trailer. Then, with a jerk, Nancy felt the trailer being lifted from its cement blocks. In the next instant the front of the trailer dropped back down.

Suddenly the trailer jerked forward, throwing Nancy and Bess backward. Josh had attached the trailer to the back of his car and was driving the trailer away—with Nancy and Bess locked inside!

15

To Catch a Thief

"Nancy, what's happening?" Bess cried as the trailer bumped along. Nancy picked herself up and, hanging on to the table for balance, helped Bess up from the floor.

"Apparently, Josh wants to get us out of the way," Nancy said grimly. "He's probably afraid someone will find us or hear us if he just left us in this trailer at the festival. And he needs time to try to get the jewels from Martine."

"I never would have thought Josh was the one doing all of this," Bess said. "He seemed like such a wimp. But now . . ." Her voice trailed off. The trailer seemed to pick up speed. "Nancy, I think he's crazy!" she cried fearfully.

Nancy reached out to squeeze Bess's hand. She didn't want to worry her friend even more, but she, too, had been wondering how far Josh would go to get the fan holder and brooch. Martine could be in real danger, as well as Nancy and Bess.

The trailer was now moving along very quickly. The girls sat on benches on either side of the table. Nancy told Bess that they should both try to concentrate on Josh's route. "It's our only way of keeping track of where we are," she said. "It doesn't seem as if we're headed toward the main entrance." They sat in silence, trying to feel the direction the trailer was moving in.

Soon the trailer began to slow down. It swung out into a right-hand turn and moved onto a smooth road. The trailer then made a quick left and went over some railroad tracks. Next the trailer swung right and began to pick up speed. Nancy felt the trailer weaving back and forth, and knew they must be on a winding road—and then a bumpy road. Finally the trailer came to a complete halt.

Within moments the front of the trailer began to rise.

"Brace yourself," Nancy said to Bess, "He's taking the trailer off the hitch." They felt the trailer drop to the ground. Nancy was slammed against the back of her bench, while Bess was thrown forward into the table. They heard Josh's car drive away. Then there was complete silence.

Nancy stood up shakily. "Bess, are you all right?" she asked.

Bess was rubbing her elbow. "My elbow hurts, but I think it's okay. It's my nerves that are shot," she said in a panicked voice. "Nancy, what are we going to do? He's left us out in the middle of nowhere!"

"Well," Nancy said, creasing her forehead in thought, "I don't think we're too far away from the festival grounds. Josh seemed to leave through some back exit, and the ride was pretty short after that. A right, a left, a right, and then a winding road. We could probably find our way back, but first we need to figure a way out of here," she said, looking around the trailer.

"But Josh locked the door from the outside," Bess pointed out.

"Hmm," Nancy said, staring at the door. "We can give it a try, anyway." Bracing one foot on the floor near the door, Nancy threw her shoulder against the trailer door. The trailer rocked a little from the force of her push, but the door wouldn't budge. She tried a few more times, but the door remained firmly locked.

"Time for plan B," Nancy said, rubbing her shoulder. She scanned the trailer.

"Do you *have* a plan B?" Bess asked hopefully.

"I might," Nancy said, pointing to a tapestry hanging on the wall. She climbed up onto the bench and tried to balance herself. Since there were no cement blocks holding up the front end, the whole trailer, including the bench, tilted to

136

the front. Bracing herself, Nancy pulled up a corner of the wall hanging, revealing a small window.

"I thought so," she said. "Most trailers have some kind of window. Apparently, Josh didn't want us to see this one."

Being careful to keep her balance, Nancy removed the tacks that held the tapestry on the wall. The wall hanging dropped to the floor. Then she tried the window. To her delight, the glass slid easily along the frame, exposing a screen. Gathering all her strength, she put both hands on the screen and pushed. It didn't budge. But after a second try the screen popped out.

"Hooray!" Nancy said in triumph. "Now let's try to get out of here."

Bess looked at the open half of the window skeptically. "I hate to tell you this, Nan, but I'll never make it through that opening," she said, shaking her head.

"Sure you will," Nancy said confidently. "I'll give it a try first, so you can see how I do it. Then I can help you down from the outside."

"What if I don't make it?" Bess said in a worried voice. "I'll be trapped in here."

"Don't worry—you'll make it," Nancy said reassuringly.

Grabbing hold of the window frame, Nancy eased one leg, then the other, through the open window, bringing herself to a sitting position on the window ledge. With her legs dangling from the window, Nancy put her palms up against the outside of the trailer to brace herself. Then she gently moved her hips through the window. As she began to slide out, she threw one hand on the window ledge for support before she finally dropped to the ground. She breathed a sigh of relief as her feet hit the dirt below.

"Okay, your turn, Bess," she called into the window from outside. Bess's head poked through the window. "Now try to put your legs through," Nancy said.

"Are you kidding?" Bess said. "I can't boost myself up," she said, her voice rising in panic.

"Just hang on to the window ledge," Nancy said. "Maybe you can come through head first."

Bess's arms came through the open window, and Bess began to pull her upper body through the small opening.

"Okay, keep coming," Nancy said, moving underneath Bess. "I'll catch you."

With the top half of her body out the window, Bess put her hands on Nancy's shoulders. Wiggling her hips, she squeezed the lower half of her body through the window. Leaning on Nancy, she pushed off the window ledge with her feet and landed safely on the ground, with Nancy holding her steady.

"Nice work," Nancy said. "Just like a gymnast."

Bess smiled. "It does feel good to be out of there. But that's about all the gymnastics I can take."

"How about some walking?" Nancy said. She looked around, trying to figure out where Josh had left them. The trailer had been parked in the dirt at the side of a quiet street. Across the street were two old warehouses that appeared to be completely deserted. "I guess we should head back down this street," Nancy suggested. "This must be the winding road we were on just before Josh stopped."

The two girls set out down the street, staying near the curb. The setting sun created an eerie glow on the empty buildings.

"Do you think Josh will come back for us soon?" Bess asked nervously.

"I think that's his plan," Nancy said. "He wants to get the fan holder and brooch away from Martine as quickly as possible. Then he'll come back for us, so we can lead him to the ring and earrings."

"Let's stay off the road, then!" Bess exclaimed, pulling Nancy over. "Who knows what Josh would do if he saw us? Don't forget—he's the one who shot an arrow at us. I don't even want to *think* about what else he's capable of doing," she added, shuddering.

"I don't think he really meant to hurt me, or anyone else, with that arrow," Nancy said. "Injuring someone wouldn't have guaranteed that he'd get the jewels back. I think the arrow, and the dagger in my front door, were only meant to scare us. Josh was probably hoping that we'd quit our volunteer jobs and turn in the jewels along with our costumes."

"Maybe," Bess said, sounding doubtful. "But I sure don't want to run into him again." They walked along in silence as the sky darkened.

"Nancy," Bess said, "what do you think Josh intended to do with us after we told him where the ring and earrings were?"

Nancy knew what Bess was thinking, but she answered calmly. "The ring and earrings are at the appraiser's. There was nothing we could have done."

"Yes, but we know everything about Josh now!" Bess exclaimed. "He'd have to make sure we wouldn't tell anyone, especially the police. And the only way he could make sure of that is by—"

Bess stopped talking abruptly as Nancy threw up her hand in warning. She was staring intently down the street. In the distance two faint spots of light could be seen. As they came closer, Nancy realized that they were headlights.

"There's a car coming, Bess," Nancy said.

"Oh, no!" Bess wailed.

Grabbing Bess's hand, Nancy began to run toward a row of old storage sheds that they'd been passing. Nancy began to look for somewhere to hide. The sheds had been built as a single unit, and there was no space in between them. Nancy realized they'd have to run to the end of the row of sheds. She looked up to see the headlights coming closer and closer.

"Bess, we have to stay as close to the sheds as we can," Nancy said. "We'll have to run to the end." They began to run, and a few moments later they rounded the corner of the last shed. Nancy paused and flattened herself against the side of the shed.

"Nancy, come on!" Bess cried. "We have to get behind the sheds!"

Nancy was watching the headlights swing around a curve in the road. The car seemed to be moving down the street very carefully. But Josh knew where the trailer was, Nancy thought. She couldn't understand why he would be driving so slowly.

As the car came out of the curve, Nancy suddenly exclaimed, "Bess! That's *my* car!" She ran out from the side of the shed into the street. Stopping in the middle of the street, she waved her arms in front of the oncoming headlights.

The blue Mustang came to a stop, and Nancy heard George's voice call out, "Nancy?"

Nancy ran around to the side of her car and greeted George with a big smile. "I don't know how you found us, but I'm sure glad you're here," she said.

Bess ran up to join them. "Oh, George, thank goodness it's you!" she cried, her face showing her obvious relief.

"What in the world happened to you two?" George asked as Nancy and Bess climbed into the car, trying to catch their breath.

"I'll tell you in a minute," Nancy said. "But first we need to hurry back to the festival. I think Martine is in trouble."

George pulled a U-turn in the deserted street and began driving back. "What's wrong?" she said.

"You first," Bess said. "What on earth are you doing here?"

George shrugged. "Well, when I didn't see you two all afternoon, I started to get a little worried. I figured you must have found out something about the jewels at the appraiser's."

"We did. They're real, all right," Bess told her cousin.

George let out a whistle. "Anyway," she continued, "when performance time rolled around, and I still hadn't heard from you, I started to look around. I saw Nancy's car near the trailer area. I went over to it and saw that the keys were still in the ignition. So I knew something was up."

"I'll say!" Bess interrupted again. "Josh kidnapped us!" she exclaimed.

"Josh?" George said in disbelief. "Is he the one who's been after the jewels?"

142

"Yes," Nancy said, "and he's going after Martine's brooch and fan holder right now. But George, how did you know where to look for us?"

George was still shaking her head in amazement. "I didn't know where to look," she said. "I knew you weren't at the festival, so I decided to try the area around the festival grounds. I've been driving around for a while. I was almost ready to give up."

"Thank goodness you didn't," Bess said gratefully.

"We owe you one," Nancy added.

"So why did Josh kidnap you?" George asked.

"He needed to get the earrings and ring from us right away," Nancy said. "He's meeting with a buyer tonight, and then he's leaving town."

As George pulled the Mustang into the festival grounds, Bess explained how she and Nancy had been locked in Josh's trailer. Nancy directed George to a parking space near the entrance. Then the three girls jumped out of the car and headed for the theater.

They walked in through the back and looked down toward the stage, where *Romeo and Juliet* had just entered its final act—the last act of the festival. The lights from the stage lit up the front row of seats, and as Nancy's eyes fell upon the front row, her heart sank. Queen Elizabeth's seat was empty. Martine wasn't there!

16

A Royal Wrap-up

"Martine's not in her seat," Nancy whispered. She pulled Bess and George away from the back row of seats.

Bess gasped. "Where could she be?" she whispered, her eyes wide with fright.

"Josh must have gotten to her before the show started," Nancy answered. "Maybe he felt he was running out of time."

"Maybe Josh took Martine off the festival grounds, like he did with you two," George spoke up. "We could do a quick search of the area," she suggested.

Nancy nodded. "Why don't you take my car, George? Bess and I will run backstage and see if anyone has seen Martine."

George immediately turned toward the parking lot, but Nancy grabbed her arm. "One more thing. There's a pay phone near the entrance. You call the police."

"Got it," George said, taking off again.

Nancy and Bess quickly made their way backstage. There was no sign of Josh under the large tent—there were just a few crew members who were busy listening to the play. As quietly as she could, Nancy moved up to the stage curtain. Suddenly she heard someone behind her whisper, "Nancy!" She turned around to see Philip Schotter, looking very worried.

"I'm glad I found you," the director said in a low voice. "Do you have any idea where Martine is? We had to start the play without her in the audience. None of the ladies-in-waiting or the courtiers know where she is. No one does," he said.

Nancy shook her head. Now she felt sure Martine was in real trouble. "What about Josh?" she asked Schotter. "Have you seen him?"

"No, I haven't," the director said, looking even more confused. "He's usually backstage during the play, but not tonight. Nancy, what do you think is going on?" he demanded.

"I'm sorry, but I just don't have time to explain right now," Nancy said, looking around her. She saw Bess approaching and waved her friend toward them. "Bess will let you know what we found out this afternoon," she said to the director. "I'll be back as soon as I can."

After telling Bess to explain everything to Schotter, Nancy then left the tent. She stopped for a moment outside the tent, thinking. If no one had been able to find Martine before the play started, then Josh must have gone after the actress while she was still preparing for the procession, she reasoned. Most likely, then, Martine would have been in her trailer. Nancy immediately set out for the trailers.

Nancy slipped quietly behind the first trailer in a row that ran alongside the woods. She listened in the darkness for sounds, but the area seemed perfectly still.

Walking cautiously between the first and second trailers, Nancy peeked around the corner, facing a long empty space separating the rows. It was hard to see in the dark, but Nancy tried. She hoped she wasn't too late.

Suddenly two figures jumped from the doorway of a trailer at the end of the second row. One of the figures had the shadowy outline of a full-length skirt and was being pushed ahead by the second figure, who wore pants. Nancy's heart skipped a beat. It had to be Martine and Josh.

Nancy came out from behind the trailer and began to creep down the aisle between the trailer rows, staying close to the trailers on one side. Her eyes were fixed on the two figures, who stopped for a moment as Josh closed the trailer door. He then began to push Martine forward. Nancy thought she could see the dagger in Josh's hand.

146

She figured he must be leading Martine toward his car. There was no time to lose.

Nancy stepped out from the shadows of the trailers and yelled, "Martine!" Instantly both figures whirled around.

Josh raised the dagger. "Hey!" he said in a surprised voice, releasing his grip on Martine.

Martine, clutching the fan holder in her hand, ran in between two trailers and slipped out of sight. Nancy found herself only a few yards away from Josh and his dagger.

Josh stood motionless for a second, looking first at Nancy and then in the direction in which Martine had run. Then he ran toward the trailers, apparently deciding to go after Martine first.

Nancy immediately took off after him. When she saw him run behind a trailer, she knew it was her last chance. She flung herself toward him in a flying tackle. Hitting him squarely in the knees, she felt him fall to the ground with a thud. From the corner of her eye she saw the dagger fly out of his hand.

"Police!" a voice called out. "Don't move!"

Relief spread over Nancy. She could hear Josh muttering under his breath. Then she saw George run up behind two police officers.

"Nancy!" George cried. "Nice tackle!"

Nancy pulled herself up with a grin.

"Thanks," she said, brushing herself off. "But I think I'll leave football to the pros."

A few moments later Nancy found herself in the backstage tent, explaining Josh's activities to the festival troupe. Every single one of them was shocked.

"I've been trying to explain to everyone that some of the jewels were real," Bess said.

Philip Schotter was shaking his head. "But I just can't believe that it was Josh Forster who had been scheming to steal them. He was my right-hand man," the director said sadly. "Once he knew the jewels were real, why didn't he just take them?" Schotter asked. "Why did he have to try to harm people?"

Nancy shook her head. "I guess he liked the way he could manipulate everyone. As a consultant, he could only suggest ideas and answer questions. But as a note writer, he made everybody sit up and take notice."

"Or fall down and take notice," Joanna Messerman put in. "I can't believe Josh was the one who made me fall off the balcony."

Nancy added, "I don't think he originally set out to hurt people. He damaged the weapons rack and Martine's litter only to get the jewels. And when he loosened the screws on the balcony and switched the rapiers, he was really trying to draw everyone's attention away from the jewels. He wanted us to focus on the acts of sabotage—not on the missing jewels—so he wrote those mysterious notes. It worked for a while," she pointed out.

"No one would have even thought about the jewels if Bess and I hadn't found them in that storage trailer," Nancy went on. "But once Bess, Martine, and I started to wear the *real* pieces—the earrings, the ring, the brooch, and the fan holder—Josh had to start all over again. He was desperate to get them back.

"That's why he tried to take the brooch from Martine's neck by strangling her," Nancy explained. "And he even tried to break into my house one night." There were a few gasps. "But he was unsuccessful both times."

Martine smiled. "A woman and her jewels aren't soon parted!" she exclaimed with a flourish. The cast and crew laughed.

"Are the jewels safe now?" Schotter asked.

Nancy nodded. "Martine has the brooch and the fan holder, and the earrings and ring Bess and I were wearing are with the appraiser."

As the troupe continued to talk among themselves, Nancy took Philip Schotter aside. "I know Martine is still a bit shaken from the last couple of hours," she said. "But she still seems to be much happier tonight. Have you noticed?"

Schotter nodded. "I think I know why. This morning she and I spoke about her contract. I reassured her that the producers and I were very happy with her performance. We agreed that Martine would have the role for a couple of years, but would set aside a few nights here and there for local actresses in certain cities to play the part."

"And Martine was satisfied with that?" Nancy asked.

Schotter nodded. "I think she really likes being the queen," he said. "It's not as demanding as a lead speaking role, and it allows her to travel and meet people and still be involved in theater—and get a lot of attention." He smiled. "She told me she was afraid that if she were forced out of the role, people would think she was getting too old to work. I don't know where she got that idea," the director said, shaking his head.

"Have you heard anything more from Louis Romero?" Nancy asked.

"Well, Dean and I have been talking about an offer Romero made to Dean," Schotter said. "He wants to have a medieval fair here next year at the same time we have the festival."

Nancy nodded. She remembered Dean's note to himself to tell the director about Romero's letter.

"Of course, Dean doesn't want to be involved

in Romero's medieval fair," Schotter said. "He doesn't think it would be a good career move for an actor. Let's just say that Romero probably isn't too interested in medieval history. Dean would probably end up operating one of the rides," he added with a wry smile.

"So why did Dean tell you about the offer if he had already decided to turn it down?" she asked.

"Dean wanted to make sure I knew that he's a sought-after actor," Schotter said, chuckling. "He thinks that will improve his chances of getting more money and publicity."

"Just as I had suspected," Nancy murmured under her breath.

Schotter grinned. "I don't think Dean will ever get as much publicity as he thinks he deserves," he observed. "And as for the money, Dean has a pretty good contract with us. He's never seriously spoken to me about changing it."

Nancy felt a tap on her shoulder. She turned around to see Bess standing next to Mrs. Pellworth. "Look who I found wandering around the festival," Bess said.

"Hello again, Mrs. Pellworth," Nancy said warmly. "It's nice to see you."

The elderly woman smiled, but she looked a little flustered. "Bess has just told me that some of my jewelry is real," she said in astonishment. "I had no idea! My goodness, I never thought for a minute that they might be authentic. Now I understand why you were asking me all those questions this afternoon," she finished.

"I didn't want to worry you," Nancy explained. "I wanted to wait until I knew more myself."

Philip Schotter stepped in. "Mrs. Pellworth, I know you donated those jewels thinking they were only costume pieces. The troupe is more than willing to return them to you."

Mrs. Pellworth smiled. "Thank you," she said graciously. "But I think those authentic pieces belong in a museum. I'd like to contact the museum curator here in River Heights and see if they would accept the donation."

"I have a feeling they'd be more than happy to accept them," Schotter said, smiling.

"It's just such a shame to think that a learned scholar like Josh Forster would resort to stealing," Mrs. Pellworth commented.

"Well, you know what they say, Mrs. Pellworth," Nancy said. "'Oh, what a tangled web we weave . . .'"

"When we're with Nancy Drew!" George and Bess finished in unison.